WINNER OF THE 2009

MARY MCCARTHY PRIZE IN SHORT FICTION

SELECTED BY DAVID MEANS

Greetings from Below

DAVID PHILIP MULLINS

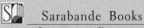 Sarabande Books
LOUISVILLE, KENTUCKY

FIRST EDITION

Managing Editor
Sarabande Books, Inc.
2234 Dundee Road, Suite 200
Louisville, KY 40205

LIBRARY OF CONGRESS CATALOGING-IN-PUBLICATION DATA

Mullins, David Philip, 1974–
  Greetings from below : stories / David Philip Mullins ; selected by David Means. — 1st ed.
      p. cm.
  ISBN 978-1-932511-88-8 (pbk. : alk. paper)
  I. Means, David, 1961– II. Title.
  PS3613.U4536G74 2010
  813'.6—dc22
                                      2010005123

Cover and text design by Kirkby Gann Tittle.

Manufactured in Canada.

This book is printed on acid-free paper.

Sarabande Books is a nonprofit literary organization.

This project is supported in part by an award from the National Endowment for the Arts.

The Kentucky Arts Council, the state arts agency, support Sarabande Books with state tax dollars and federal funding from the National Endowment for the Arts.

for Seraphim—who else?

. . . as this appalling ocean surrounds the verdant land, so in the soul of man there lies one insular Tahiti, full of peace and joy, but encompassed by all the horrors of the half known life.

—Herman Melville, *Moby-Dick*

CONTENTS

ACKNOWLEDGMENTS

The stories in this book have appeared, in slightly different form, in the following publications:

Cimarron Review ("A Familiar Place")

Ecotone ("Arboretum")

Fiction ("Longing to Love You," as "The Last Thing in the World")

Folio ("Crash Site on a Desert Mountain Outside Las Vegas")

The Massachusetts Review ("Glitter Gulch")

New England Review ("Driving Lessons"; "True Love Versus the Cigar-Store Indian"; "First Sight")

The Yale Review ("This Life or the Next")

I would like to thank the following editors for their faith and guidance: Ben George, Clay Matthews, Andrew Lieb, Sean Santa, David Lenson, Liz Harris Behling, and J.D. McClatchy. I would especially like to thank Stephen Donadio, longtime editor of *New England Review*, for taking a chance on me back in 2000; if he hadn't, I may have given up.

Many thanks to the folks at the Sewanee Writers' Conference—most notably, Don Waters, Margot Livesey, and Randall Kenan—as well as to everyone at Yaddo, where a part of this book was written. Thanks, too, to my friends and teachers from the Iowa Writers' Workshop, particularly James Alan McPherson, Chris Offutt, Marilynne Robinson, ZZ Packer, Thisbe Nissen, Ethan Canin, James Hynes, Jim Crace, Connie Brothers, Jan Zenisek, Deb West, and Frank Conroy.

For their belief in my work and for their tireless efforts to see it published, thank you to Nat Sobel, Julie Stevenson, Cate Peebles, and everyone else at Sobel Weber Associates, Inc.

Huge props to all those who critiqued early, execrable drafts of these stories, including Christian Brebbia, Neil Evans, Adena Williams, Matthew Vollmer, Amy Grace Loyd, and Ian Stansel. My heartfelt gratitude for the time and input. A very special thank you to John Irsfeld, one of the most generous human beings I've ever known, for patiently editing almost every sentence of fiction I've ever written and for eighteen long years of coaching and encouragement.

For various acts of kindness, big old thanks to Rick Moody, Joyce Carol Oates, Jack Brebbia, Teri Tobias, and Rachel Donadio. Thanks also to Lisa Lenzo and Jamie Enus for serendipitous inspiration.

Thank you to David Means for selecting this book for the Mary McCarthy Prize, as well as to Sarah Gorham and the rest of the Sarabande team for handling it with care.

For support, motivation, and, most importantly, love, I owe thanks to my mother, Marie Mullins, and to Flemming Loevenvig. I also owe thanks to my father, Jim Mullins, for inculcating me with a respect for literature and for keeping a copy of *Raise High the Roof Beam, Carpenters and Seymour: An Introduction* in his sock drawer—finding it changed my life forever.

My eternal appreciation to Zoey and James, for giving me a reason to believe in our species and for making me try harder in everything I do.

Finally, the biggest thank you of all to my loving wife, Seraphim, whom I owe everything I have. Without her companionship, sacrifices, editorial insight, and unending aplomb, this book could never have been written.

D.P.M.

Foreword

To find a beautiful collection of stories in a pile of
manuscripts is, for any judge of any contest, a wonderful surprise, a
kind of revelatory experience. This comes in part from knowing—
as most writers know—that a good short story is a balancing act, a
tightrope walk of innumerable elements all working together for a
short duration to draw out and reveal a particular mystery. It's one
thing to read a good story in a magazine, singular and alone, but it's
another to find an entire book of them, fully realized, each one honed
to perfection, neat and tidy, into a collection that holds together like
one of those great pop albums of yore, producing a cohesive aesthetic
experience. What a pleasure to find not only a strong collection of
stories, but a distinctive voice, clear and precise, and a vision that is
unique and new while at the same time rooted in the traditions of
the form, echoing Ernest Hemingway, Frank O'Connor, Flannery
O'Connor, and all of the other great practitioners who took the
risk of writing short fiction. As Frank O'Connor pointed out, each
attempt at writing a story contains "the possibility of a new form as
well as a possibility of a complete fiasco."

Well, David Philip Mullins risked a fiasco and instead created a highly original collection of short stories. Mullins understands that inventiveness arises from acute attention to the demands of each story and respect for the material itself. Every writer finds a way into the work: Chekhov leaned close and, with his ear cupped, caught the intimate conversations between lovers—and serfs and masters—watching them move in what seemed to be isolated chambers of their desires. Borges sealed himself into a diving bell of his own fantastic style, plunging deep into seas of time and culture. Alice Munro maps expansive topographies of relationships, mostly female, using her utterly and deceptively unique style to reveal the complex meeting points of personal history, geography, and destiny. And Mullins, for his part, gently threads the narrative of a single character through a hole of paternal loss, watching carefully as he passes through early boyhood up through adulthood (and we're talking real adulthood, not the delayed adolescence so common in the culture today), uncovering in each story something about the mystery in the connection between the loss of a father and the formation of a sexual identity. The originality here is not the loud kind—stylistic high jinks, flashy explosive plots—but rather the quiet kind that comes from deep thought, from an impulse to tweeze apart the experiences found in the life of a character named Nick Danze.

Another great pleasure in this book comes from discovering David Philip Mullins's own, unique Las Vegas—not the Las Vegas of so many movies and books (a hardcore playpen of debauchery and sin) or the Las Vegas of Hunter Thompson (the cold center of the dead American dream), but rather a city as seen from the vantage of a typical suburban kid looking through scrub and grass at the lights, feeling the magnetic draw of cheap thrills from afar. Throughout this collection the city shifts and changes as Nick matures. He moves in close, tempted by its allure, but never gives in to it as his mother does.

And because we are moving alongside him, we're given a huge gift: a new perspective on a place we thought we knew.

Don't be fooled by the cool, clear voice of these stories. Mullins, like most good story writers, is by nature deeply subversive, unwilling to look away, voyeuristic in his impulse to glance through the keyhole at the action behind the door, risky in his willingness to once more take on the theme of male experience. I'm grateful to him for giving the world an indelible, unforgettable character. Far into the future, where literature will continue to live, many readers will be grateful, too.

—David Means

Greetings from Below

Arboretum

THE SAPLINGS STOOD IN NEAT ROWS ALONG EASTERN AVENUE, each leafless maple growing from a dark hump of soil that resembled a pitcher's mound, or a small grave. They rose six, seven feet above the sidewalk. With flashlights and a trowel, we uprooted the shortest one we could find and carried it off to our plywood fort in the desert. I was in my early teens. It was late on a Sunday, and I had left my house in the middle of the night without permission. Surrounded by catclaws and schist rocks, the fort was a rickety structure that sat stark and uninviting in the middle of a dried-up arroyo. Kilburg had said that all the outside needed was a little greenery, a few trees.

Earlier that evening, I had learned that my father was going to die, and I was glad to be out in the open, away from home. Kilburg had convinced me to sneak out my bedroom window, to meet him at the end of our block at a quarter past eleven. Now he had me on my hands and knees, scooping rocks and hard-packed dirt baked solid after a rainless winter. The drought that had begun in December had yet to subside. This was more than twenty-five years ago, before interstate water banking, and people joked that their faucets might soon run dry. Summer was two months away, but even out at the fort—a twenty-minute walk into the Mojave wilderness that bordered our neighborhood to the south—the warm air had begun to smell of the chlorinated swimming pools and freshly mowed lawns that were partially at fault for the city's water shortage. Beside me Kilburg massaged his aching stump. He could only stand for so long before he had to remove his prosthetic leg, a hollow, plastic thing, a mannequin's appendage, from which he sometimes drank the Bushmills whiskey I borrowed from my father's liquor cabinet.

"I don't know about you, but I sure could use some action," said Kilburg. The leg lay beneath him in the dirt; he sat crouched on it as though it were a log at a campfire. It had once matched the color of his skin but had faded to an unnatural ivory. In one hand he held a flashlight, and with the other he kneaded his stump in a slow figure eight, avoiding the spot in the center where the skin had been knotted together like the end of a hot dog.

"Action?" I asked. I scooped a clump of dirt over my shoulder and it hit the ground like a stale dinner roll. "What kind of action?"

The sapling was propped against the overturned paint bucket we used as a bongo drum. Behind us the fort stood at an angle, leaning westward, undeserving of its name: it wasn't fortified in any way and appeared on the verge of collapse. Deep in what seemed an uncharted region of the Mojave—there were no trails, no cigarette butts or empty beer bottles left behind by the local high-school kids who partied in the desert—and concealed by the arroyo's high, crumbling banks, it was at least unknown to the rest of the world. Building the fort had been Kilburg's idea. We had spent an entire Saturday wrestling with the sheets of plywood we had found in his father's tool shed, shaping a door frame with his ancient jigsaw and dragging the sheets one by one through the desert to hammer them together, and in the end our construction was nothing more than four unpainted walls and a low, flat roof, less complex than your average doghouse.

Kilburg shook his head at the ground, the way he did whenever I asked him a question.

"*Action*," he said. "*Chicks*. Jesus, do I have to explain everything?"

"Oh," I said, and felt like an idiot.

Travis Kilburg was tall and muscular, with long earlobes and a wide, open face. He wore a military buzz cut, and it seems to me now that his complexion always had a greenish tint to it—like the patina of an old bronze statue—his eyes dark and serious. Kilburg had diabetes and had lost his leg at the age of six due to a blocked artery. He liked to talk about sex, about the many girls whose virginity he had taken, though I knew that he himself was a virgin. We both were. We were fourteen years old. Neither of us had ever even kissed anyone. Kilburg was perhaps incapable of honesty, no matter what the topic, and I played along when he fabricated his exploits, nodding as he spun tales of seduction and conquest.

I stabbed the trowel into the dirt, leaning to grab a few pebbles from the hole. I didn't mind doing all the work. It took my thoughts off the news my parents had delivered over dinner. According to my father's doctor, a rare lung condition—a fibrosis—was responsible for his chronic cough, for his labored breathing, which in the last couple of months had grown louder and raspier. "Talk to him, Jack," my mother said. "He has a right to know." My father explained that his lungs were in bad shape, their tissue inflamed. Without at least one transplant, he told me, swallowing the words as he chewed, the fibrosis could prove fatal. "*Will*," my mother corrected him, "*will* prove fatal. We just want you to understand what's going on, Nick." The only person I had ever known to die had been my grandfather on my mother's side, who'd had a heart attack two summers earlier. After a long silence my mother suggested we move to California, near the Scripps Research Institute in La Jolla. My father's doctor, a general practitioner, had told them that the respiratory specialists there were among the foremost in the world. Tearfully, my mother reminded my father that because of his age—forty-three—his name would be placed near the bottom of a long waiting list for a new lung. He needed a specific kind of treatment. A move to the coast, she said, might prolong his life, might save it. My father lowered his eyes toward his plate. He reminded my mother that Las Vegas was our home.

"You bring the booze?" Kilburg said now. He put a licked finger to the air. "It's about that time."

"Just some schnapps."

The liter of Bushmills I had borrowed in the past had been half-empty, and tonight I had chosen a bottle of DeKuyper Peachtree instead, paranoid that my father might have secretly taken to watching the volume of his whiskey. I had a hunch that Kilburg might declare the schnapps an unacceptable offering, but he only shrugged and said, "Whatever, man. Booze is booze."

I held the sapling up to the light. Dark soil clung to a knot of roots. A shiny worm writhed from the soil, twisting around like a periscope. I positioned the roots in the hole and scooped the dirt back in, patting it flat around the trunk.

"There," I said. "What do you think?"

Like the fort, the sapling leaned heavily to one side, in a way that made it look pathetic.

"Just as I pictured it," he said. "This place looks better already. When that thing grows leaves, we'll have ourselves a little color out here." He kneaded his stump harder now, as though working a knotted muscle. "Well, what are you waiting for? Let's celebrate."

I reached into my back pocket and brought around the bottle of schnapps, a pint. I handed it to Kilburg, and he uncapped it and sniffed the contents. He made a face, crinkling his nose, then caught himself and smiled. "Just what the doctor ordered," he said. "All we need are some chicks and we'd have a party on our hands."

"Tell me about it."

He took a long pull, wincing as he lowered the bottle. Kilburg rarely discussed his health, and at the time I wasn't sure if having diabetes meant that he shouldn't be drinking. I had never seen him test his blood sugar or inject insulin, nor had I ever thought of his illness as life-threatening. He seemed, at any rate, to have a high tolerance for alcohol, or pretended to. Kilburg would do almost anything for attention. Just above the knee joint, his prosthetic leg opened into a kind of cup, and it was from here that he would drink my father's whiskey. Into the cup fit a concave socket, attached to which was a leather sleeve that laced up like a shoe. The sleeve slid snugly over his stump—the stump resting inside the padded socket—and when the laces were tied the leg was supposed to remain attached. But if Kilburg took a clumsy step as we crossed the uneven terrain of the desert, the socket would come out, popping like a cork, and he would pitch forward into the dirt. What's more, the knee and ankle joints—crude-looking mechanisms that bent in accordance with a complicated arrangement of pins and bearings— creaked when he walked, and his stump itched and perspired and developed weekly blisters, causing him to grimace and complain. He moved with the lopsided gait of an arthritic old man. At school, kids tormented him, particularly Todd Sheehan and Chad Klein, two boys in our class who wore baseball caps and chewed tobacco. They were thuggish and athletic-looking—as big as Kilburg—and they called him Peg Leg and Gimp, tripping him whenever they had the chance. Even so, I thought, back then, that there were other, smaller kids on whom Kilburg took out his frustration.

"College chicks," he said, taking another pull. "That's what we really need."

We were still in junior high school, and I wondered if Kilburg had ever even met a college-aged woman.

"I'd go to UNLV for the chicks alone," he offered, "but my dad says college is for people who think they're too good to work."

Kilburg was the son of a chemical-plant operator, and he often found a way to incorporate his father's opinions into a conversation. He was determined to follow in the man's footsteps, to land himself a job someday at Kerr-McGee, where his father had worked for the past twenty years. Perhaps because my own father was an engineer, Kilburg needled me about being what he called a "richie," even though we lived in a small single-story house just up the block. Both our fathers worked in the desert, but the Kerr-McGee plant was only twenty minutes outside the city. The nuclear test site where my father worked was over an hour away.

Three years earlier, Kilburg's mother had run off with a gambler from Arizona, a man she had met at a poker table. As a consequence, it occurs to me now, Kilburg liked to brag that he had the coolest father in the neighborhood—the smartest and the toughest. His father was tall and potbellied, and he glared at you with stony eyes, and when he spoke his black beard parted to reveal a mouth full of crooked teeth, many of which overlapped or were angled to such a degree that you could see their rotting undersides. Evenings, he nursed a Heineken in his Barcalounger until he fell asleep. Kilburg worshipped him, but on more than one occasion he had shown up for school with a fat lip, or a bruised cheekbone, or a cut above his eye. When I had asked Kilburg, the Monday after we had built the fort, why his wrist was black-and-blue, he told me that a stereo speaker had fallen on him—knocked over by Tarkanian, his German shepherd—but I suspected the injury had been punishment for the wood that had gone missing from his father's shed.

Presently, Kilburg switched off the flashlight, slipping it into a pocket of his shorts. "C'mon," he said. He handed me the bottle, scooting himself off the prosthetic leg and onto the ground, his real leg stretched out in front of him. Pushing with his hands, the same way we eased ourselves down the sloping banks of the arroyo, he inched across the dirt and into the fort.

I crawled behind him through the low door frame. A green shag rug, taken from a supermarket Dumpster, covered the hard dirt floor. Flashlights hung like inverted torches in each of the four corners, dangling upside down from shoestrings nailed to the plywood, one of the bulbs always faintly flickering. Brushing against a wall of the fort caused the flashlights to sway in their corners, yellow beams criss-crossing the rug as if it were a dance floor. Each month Kilburg stole the latest issue of *Playboy* from the 7-Eleven near our school, and our only adornment was a glossy centerfold of Bernadette Peters, thumb-tacked to the wall opposite the door frame.

I took a sip of the schnapps, coughing as it burned down my throat.

"There you go," he laughed. He took off his shoe, a white sneaker whose mate was outside, on the foot of the prosthetic leg. "We'll make a man outta you yet."

Before long I had a terrific buzz going. My head had grown numb, and I was loose-jointed, slurring my speech. The two of us lay flat on the rug. In the still air I could smell sagebrush and Kilburg's cheap drugstore cologne. He kept saying, "You drunk yet? You feeling anything?" I pinched my eyes closed and a kaleidoscope of color spun behind the lids. When I opened them, Kilburg was leaning over me, his breath warm on my face.

"Get off," I said, squirming, but he held my arms. I couldn't get free, pinned by the stiff weight of his torso. I looked away. Through the door frame I could see the moon, white light in a black sky. When he put his lips to mine, I let out a grumble, doubtful of my sudden arousal, a tingling sensation that rained from the crown of my head to the tips of my fingers. I was confused, unsure of how to process what was happening, but he slipped his tongue into my mouth, and I found myself giving in to the kiss. He eased off me, touching my ears, my cheeks, the side of my neck. Then he forced his stump into my hip, and gave a shudder when my erection brushed against his own. What we were doing seemed wrong—criminal, maybe—but I started to feel energized, bold, the way I had felt when we had stolen the sapling from Eastern Avenue, the way I imagined Kilburg felt when he shoplifted *Playboy*s from 7-Eleven. I brought my arm up around his neck, but he batted it away.

"Easy, lover boy," he said. He rolled off me, laughing.

"I thought—"

"*I thought, I thought*," he mocked. "Relax. We're not fags, dude. It's only practice for the real thing, for when we both get girlfriends." Kilburg narrowed his eyes as if the answer to a troublesome question had finally dawned on him. "We're drunk, Nick. We're not thinking right. Don't ever tell anybody about this." He pulled his shoe back on, looking panicky. "You do and you're a dead man."

My father began taking a daily dose of prednisone, a steroid meant to decrease the inflammation in his lungs. Local specialists struggled to slow the fibrosis they said would take his life, guessing that overexposure to unsafe chemicals at the test site had been its cause. I didn't know why it was that Kilburg's father, who worked at a chemical plant, didn't suffer from a fibrosis of his own. My mother kept me updated on the specifics of my father's condition. Over the past several weeks he had undergone a CAT scan and a bronchoscopy—procedures I had never heard of—and already there seemed to be a lack of hope in his eyes, as if he had predicted the ultimate uselessness of his treatment. How long did he have to live? And what exactly was a fibrosis, anyway? The word itself was a mystery. What would be my father's last requests, and what would life be like without him? Such questions troubled me but were often replaced by daydreams of being at the fort with Kilburg.

We continued to sneak out after dark, the course of each night the same. We hid behind the corner of an office building, or in the shadows of an empty strip mall, peering from the darkness until the coast was clear, waiting as motorists made their way up and down the avenue. To the trill of katydids—everywhere that spring—we dug a twiglike sapling from the earth, wrapped its roots in a plastic produce bag, and made our way by flashlight into the desert. After planting a sapling, we saturated the ground with water we brought in plastic thermoses, and in a chrome flask my father kept in his liquor cabinet. Later, we drank ourselves to recklessness, finding new ways of expressing our attraction: petting, unzipping, fondling, going farther every time, Kilburg always in control. I concocted elaborate fantasies during which we spent entire weekends together, waking on the shag rug, unclothed in each other's arms. Prior to our first kiss, I had never thought of him or any other male in such a manner. But my desire for Kilburg quickly grew as strong as any I'd had for a girl, and all the more surprising, I suppose, for the fact that he had only one leg.

To girls I was invisible, a brainy kid with chronic acne, buck-toothed and exceedingly thin. To Kilburg I was worth something. Not a day went by when I didn't think about him. I felt lucky to be more than just his friend, though I was convinced I wasn't gay, decid-ing on a precise distinction between bona fide homosexuality and my curious interest in Travis Kilburg. Surely a person could be drawn, temporarily at least, to a member of the same sex without being a homosexual—surely there were explanations for such a phenome-non. Like Kilburg, I didn't want anyone to know about what we did at the fort.

By the end of May—as the days grew longer and the air dryer, the sun scorching the valley with what people now joked could only be malice—the saplings numbered twelve around the fort. After dinner my father read from newspaper articles about the drought, the longest in the city's history, his voice thin and scratchy as he shook his head in disbelief. His hands had fattened from the prednisone and had taken on a yellowish color, as though he soaked them in formaldehyde. One evening he ran across an article that made mention of the missing maples. "Whoever's taking those trees should be rewarded," he said, calling our crime retribution for the city's mistake of planting them in the first place, in the middle of a drought. He was right. It had been a surprising decision, and you got the feeling that, drought or no drought, the city was trying to change the landscape of Las Vegas, trying to turn it into something it wasn't. The saplings were well-hidden at the fort, but I worried that the avenue might now be under some kind of twenty-four-hour surveillance. When I mentioned this to Kilburg, it seemed only to excite him. "Screw 'em," he said. "Bring 'em on."

Mornings, we walked together to school—through our neighborhood and up Eastern Avenue, past each of the humps of soil we had emptied, caved-in like little volcanoes—but when I ran into Kilburg between classes, he usually ignored me. Todd Sheehan and Chad Klein teased him as he hobbled through the hallways, and time after time I had the urge to stand up for him. I never did, afraid they might unleash their viciousness on me.

My mother, who worked days as a receptionist but played the violin in her spare time, started speaking of my father as though he were already dead, her words bearing a gravity that seemed childish and contrived. "Before long, it'll just be the two of us," she would say with tear-filled eyes, playing something morose by Brahms or Tchaikovsky—composers she spoke of as if they were friends—lowering her head and sawing away at the strings, her hand moving wildly up and down the fingerboard. She had always thought of herself as an artist whose potential had never fully developed. Resting the bow on her shoulder, she would tell me to get used to being the man of the house, and hand me a tissue. When I failed to cry, she would insist that I was in a state of denial. But if my father was around, my mother was all smiles, preparing his favorite meals, surprising him with tickets to a movie or a new set of golf clubs. She bought him watches, ties, books by his favorite authors, and in June, for his forty-fourth birthday, she gave him a new Buick LeSabre—an expense, I know now, my parents couldn't afford.

One night when I returned home from the fort, a light was on in the family room. It was late, one o'clock. I had never been caught sneaking out, and I feared that my parents had finally discovered my absence. I worried the police had been called, but when I crept to the window, squinting into a space of light where the curtains didn't quite meet, I saw only my mother, her knees drawn to her chest in my father's leather armchair. She paged through a stack of sheet music, a pencil behind her ear, eyes half-closed.

I knelt down between some shrubs. My mother rested the stack of sheet music in her lap, rubbing her eyes with her knuckles. A tear streamed past the corner of her mouth as she scribbled something into a margin. When she glanced up, I ducked below the edge of the window, holding my breath. But as I looked back in—cautiously, my heart hammering in my chest—I saw her paging through the stack again. For some reason, I kept holding my breath, thinking of my father, of what it would be like to struggle for air. I thought about what the specialists had told him, that soon he would need an oxygen tank to breathe, one he would wear all the time, as you might eyeglasses or a hearing aid. I imagined tending to him, what my mother would have to go through, fretting at the bedside of a dying spouse. I, too, began to cry, ashamed of the tears, as if my father himself were my witness. Kilburg had once told me that crying was a sign of weakness, that, according to his father, shedding tears meant you were no stronger than a little girl. I had never seen my own father cry, not even when he talked about his health—which he did only when motivated by my mother—or when he wheezed around the house, huffing his words when he spoke. My chest heaved, and I let go my breath. We had parted only minutes ago, but I suddenly missed Kilburg. I didn't know if he could understand what I was feeling, but I missed him anyway, as though I might never see him again.

Placing the stack of sheet music on the floor, my mother got up from the chair, stretched her arms, and switched off the light. I walked down the block, but Kilburg's bedroom window was dark. He lived in a big split-level with wood trim and aluminum siding, out of place in our neighborhood of low stuccoed houses. As always, a trailered boat took up the driveway, and an orange '67 Mustang was parked against two bricks in the middle of the yard. A single agave grew beside the rusted automobile, the dead grass a sunburned brown. The development dipped along a hillside, and the distant valley was a bowl of glimmering light, the Strip a reddish flare that blazed across the land.

I walked around the side of the house, through the open wrought-iron gate. The backyard had never been landscaped, and patches of creosote grew from the wind-blown dirt. Along the edge of the cinderblock wall stood an abandoned lawn mower, two of its wheels missing. I sat down in an old blue wheelbarrow that was overgrown with dandelions and quack grass, as if, like the lawn mower, it hadn't moved in a hundred years. It was a school night, but I remained in the wheelbarrow for a long while, deciphering constellations that glared in the night sky, a skill my father had taught me. Kilburg was asleep in his bedroom, and I wondered if he even liked me, or anyone else, for that matter. He was a bully, and bullies weren't known to enjoy the company of others. I had never seen him completely naked, but I pictured what he might look like—a solid torso, two arms and a leg—and I unzipped my shorts and began to masturbate.

The following morning I was running late for school. When Kilburg knocked on the front door, my mother told him to go ahead without me. Fifteen minutes later, I was making my way up Eastern Avenue when I spotted him at the corner. He should have been in class by now, but there he was, twenty yards away, surrounded by Sheehan and Klein and a third boy named Billy Walsh, who had been in my gym class the previous semester. Suddenly Sheehan swung at Kilburg, clipping him on the cheek. When Kilburg raised an elbow to shield himself, Klein took a step forward and kneed him in the groin. Walsh stood in the background, howling and stomping his heel on the concrete. Doubled over, Kilburg stumbled to the left, then to the right. I waited for his leg to come off. Like a felled tree, he tipped slowly to one side, his textbooks spilling from his arms as he hit the sidewalk.

I was half a mile from school, and I considered running for help, cutting unseen through the desert and summoning the principal, Mr. Gerhard. I wondered what, if anything, Kilburg had done to provoke the boys. Walsh was short and skinny, a loudmouth and a tagalong. Paralyzed with fear, I knelt behind a beat-up Impala, figuring that, if I had to, I could take him in a fistfight. But I had recently chipped both my front teeth during a game of touch football, and I imagined Sheehan and Klein kicking them in entirely while Walsh held me from behind.

It was a hot, clear morning, and sunlight glinted off the Impala's chrome bumper. As I leaned against it, I understood that Kilburg was really no bully at all. He was just a kid with a difficult homelife and an unfair disadvantage, someone to feel sorry for. Perhaps this, beyond his physical appeal, was what I liked most about him. I suppose I loved him, or thought I did—I had never known such love, or anything like it—and I waited to feel compelled to rush to his defense, to act as any good friend would. But the feeling never came. I had once seen my father break up a quarrel between two rowdy fans at a UNLV basketball game, and I contemplated why it was that I hadn't inherited his bravery. I was glad I hadn't walked to school with Kilburg. I had nothing but a desire to escape, a spineless longing to be somewhere else: back home, or safe at the fort.

I peeked around the bumper of the Impala, holding my breath the way I had in front of my house the night before. Traffic whooshed by on the avenue. Some cars had slowed during the commotion, but none of the drivers had got out to help. Kilburg groped around on the sidewalk, trying to stand, but before he could get to his feet, Walsh did something I'll never forget. He bent down and pulled off Kilburg's leg, spitting into the leather sleeve and then tossing the leg as far down the sidewalk as he could, far enough that Kilburg would have to crawl to retrieve it.

Kilburg lay curled on the concrete as the three boys, whooping and high-fiving, made off with his textbooks. I watched him struggle to sit up, then drag himself over to the leg. As though he had sensed my presence, he looked up the avenue a few times, directly at the Impala, or so it seemed, squinting as he held his groin. Every part of me wanted to help him as I should have sooner, but if I revealed myself now he would know I had been watching all along. And so I remained behind the Impala, hidden and ashamed, as Kilburg wiped the sleeve clean with the palm of his hand, reattached the leg, and limped off toward home.

He never did show up at school, and when I called his house in the afternoon there was no answer. That night I found him at the fort. He was sitting outside, rubbing his stump in his usual way, the prosthetic leg resting beside him in the dirt. Inside, the flashlights were on, a bright glow spreading from the door frame. The air smelled strongly of marijuana.

"What are you doing here?" I asked him.

Dime-sized welts rose from his neck and arms, as though he had been pelted with stones. He had a black eye, and the side of his face, badly bruised, looked like the palm of a catcher's mitt.

"What are *you* doing here?" he said.

I sat down next to him. It seemed that not all of his injuries could have resulted from what had happened that morning, that some of them must have been his father's doing. I didn't know how to ask him if it was true that the man beat him.

"What happened to you?" I said.

He relit a joint, shaking his head as he looked down at the leg. The laces had come untied, he claimed, and he had tumbled down a flight of stairs at the school library. He had gone there, he told me, to check out a few books on gardening, since all of the saplings we had planted appeared to have died. There were fifteen in all. Many had begun to sprout leaves, but now the leaves hung from their branches like rolled parchment. There had been no end to the drought, and the water we had brought to the fort hadn't been enough to keep the maples alive.

"Jeez," I said. I felt a revulsion for myself, regret that churned in my gut. "You look pretty bad."

"Thanks," he said. "I'll heal."

"Did it hurt? The fall, I mean. You in any pain?"

"You're such a wuss," he said, and raised an eyebrow. He took a hit off the joint. "I bet you never even jerk off."

I wasn't sure what being a wuss had to do with masturbating, but I answered, "Sure I do. Who doesn't?"

"Girls don't." He handed me the joint, burned down to nothing. "Girls don't have peckers, stupid."

"Well, yeah," I said. "OK."

I had smoked marijuana only once before, with a cousin at a family reunion in Illinois. I inhaled, pinching the joint between my thumb and index finger, the way I had been shown.

"Good stuff," I ventured, managing not to cough.

Kilburg strummed an air guitar. In a rock 'n' roll falsetto, he began to sing: "*What I want, you've got, and it might be hard to handle. But like the flame that burns the candle, the candle feeds the flame.*" It was a song we both liked—"You Make My Dreams," by Hall and Oates. In a short while, my eyelids grew heavy and a dense heat surrounded me. I had a sense of time passing slowly. I was suddenly very hungry.

"*You make my dreams come true,*" he sang.

"Awesome," I said, and laughed.

He lowered his arms and took a breath. "Holy shit," he said. "I'm so goddamn stoned."

For a few seconds, neither of us spoke. The sun had set hours ago, but it had to be close to ninety degrees outside. I could feel warmth rising through the desert floor. A cloud of smoke hovered above the fort, drifting into the night as I extinguished the joint against the side of a rock. Kilburg started mumbling to himself, gesturing with his hands. I couldn't make out the words. Already my forehead was throbbing, and I was glad I hadn't taken a second hit. After a time, I heard him say, "I'm gonna fuck you."

Just like that, my high was gone, or I thought it was. "Yeah," he said, as though he had reflected on it and made up his mind. He spoke slowly, leaning back on his elbows, his voice soft but emphatic: "I'm going to fuck you."

A coyote wailed in the distance, the desert aglow in the milky light of a full moon. I had understood him well enough, and for a few weeks now I had been disturbingly curious about intercourse between men. Still, I wasn't entirely sure what he had in mind. I should have voiced my unease, but I wanted to follow his orders, whatever they might be.

"Stand up," he said, louder now. "Pull down your shorts."

I did as I was told, standing in front of him with my shorts and underwear bunched at my ankles. I felt the twinges of an erection, and soon it was bobbing beneath the hem of my T-shirt. In a corner of my mind I could see into the future, into tomorrow or next week, when I would look back and yearn for this moment. I knew that it would seem distant, fictional. I guess I was scared, but I wanted to savor it.

"Kneel down," Kilburg told me, and I knelt before him. He sat up straight, his real leg outstretched in the dirt. He took my hands in his, and his thumbs trembled in my palms. He was just as scared as I was. The muscles flexed in his arms, while a purple vein bulged from the side of his neck. He tightened his grip, squeezing until it hurt. Then he grabbed hold of my head and pushed it into his crotch. He leaned over and put his lips to my ear. "First you're gonna blow me," he whispered.

I unzipped his cutoffs, resting my cheek against his knee, where I could smell the sharp scent of his groin. I heard him take a deep, eager breath, but when I kissed the inside of his stump, tasting the salt of his skin, he flinched, pushing hard at my shoulder. I looked up at him. In the light from the door frame, he was working his jaw like an animal. It seemed as if he might vomit.

"Get away from me," he said, his face twisted in anger.

"What is it?" I said. Still kneeling, I smiled in a way that I thought might comfort him, but I only got him angrier.

"I'm not like you!" he yelled. "You make me want to throw up. You make me hate myself."

"You don't mean that."

"Just shut up," he said, pressing his fingers into his eyes. "Jesus Christ."

I pulled up my underwear and my shorts and sat back down in the dirt. I looked through the darkness, and it struck me that all across Las Vegas, at that very moment, there were people having sex. When I had turned twelve, my father had tried to broach the subject of intercourse, uncomfortably explaining that, beyond the fulfillment of desire, it was an act of love. But right now people were doing it in motel rooms and bathrooms and parked cars and storage closets, and they either loved each other or they didn't. I wasn't sure if it made any difference. It was possible that simply being with someone—anyone—was enough, and I had the idea that desire was nothing more than a form of desperation.

"I promise not to tell anyone," I said, sounding helpless. "I wouldn't ever do that." I considered taking off my shirt. To make my chest look more feminine, I had plucked what few hairs I'd had from around my nipples, and I wanted to show him. I wanted Kilburg to see what I had done. "Trav," I pleaded.

"I told you to shut up," he said, zipping his cutoffs. He pinched the knotted center of his stump, the way I had seen my father pinch the bridge of his nose when, late at night in his study, he thumbed through blueprints in preparation for the next day's work. I'm not sure what made me do it, but when Kilburg closed his eyes, as if he were trying to recall some vital piece of information, I told him my father was sick. "He's going to die," I said. "I don't know why I'm telling you this."

I was crying again, the second time in two days. I remembered what Kilburg's father had told him about shedding tears, and I felt silly and weak. Kilburg stared at his hands, his arms loose across his lap. His mother had left him without notice, and I wondered if he cried over her when no one was around.

"I already heard," he said, his voice trailing off. "My dad told me."

Between low clouds I could see the stars. They seemed to float through the sky like distant aircrafts, flashing in and out of sight, faint in the light of the moon. I thought of them falling in slow motion, all at once—a blizzard of stars—down through the universe and into the valley, filling it up before melting into the dry landscape. I assumed my mother had gone around telling everyone in the neighborhood about my father's condition, looking for pity, or who knows what. For a couple of minutes, there was only the noise of katydids, a steady chirr that filled the air. As I watched what I thought might be cumulonimbus clouds—a term I had heard my father use when he read aloud from articles about the drought—a breeze picked up, stirring dirt around the fort. The clouds came swiftly together, dark and swollen, padding the sky. I thought of the smell of sagebrush when it rained— it was hard to forget, at once fragrant and repellent, something like the smell of your hand after you licked it. Kilburg nodded his head. He seemed to have calmed down. He bent forward and picked up a rock, chucking it into the night.

"Why didn't you help me this morning?" he said.

I wiped tears from my face, looking him up and down.

"I know you were there. I saw you." He lifted his chin. "I saw you behind that car."

I tried to think of a lie—an excuse for why I hadn't defended him, to make up for the ugly truth of my cowardice—but I didn't want to hurt him any more than I already had. He pulled a flashlight from his pocket, switching it on and shining it at a yucca, a Joshua tree. Heads of sagebrush rose up among the catclaws and schist rocks. He pointed the flashlight at a small cluster of jimsonweed, swathed by little white flowers shaped like trumpets. He circled the weed with the beam, clicking his tongue.

"If you wanted to hallucinate," he said, "you could eat those flowers. Problem is, they might kill you."

"I'm sorry," I told him.

And I was. I owed him an explanation. But I was still thinking about my father. It would turn out that my father would suffer for seven more years, never undergoing a transplant yet slipping in and out of long, miraculous periods of remission, his lungs dissipating intermittently. He would die, with little warning, in a hospital room on a cold Las Vegas evening in November, a week before Thanksgiving—two years before my mother's emotional constitution would begin to unravel in earnest. At that moment, however, sitting there with Kilburg, I had a sense of imminent tragedy. In my mind, as in my mother's, my father was already dead. I pictured his last, gasping moments, then his wake: he lay in an open casket, done up with cosmetics to resemble the living, the way my grandfather had lain at his own wake two summers earlier. I saw Kilburg beside me at the burial, and afterward—days later, perhaps—I saw the two of us sneaking into the cemetery at night and, in my father's memory, planting a sapling behind his headstone. I saw Travis Kilburg as an important part of my life, even though I felt that this would be our last time together at the fort—that we would never steal another sapling, that our relationship was more or less over. Indeed, we would never go back to the fort again. Kilburg would eventually move across town, and the last time I would run into him would be at a party the week before I would leave home for college, where he would tell me he dropped out of school and took an entry-level job his father got him at the Kerr-McGee plant. It would be an awkward conversation, but I would have no feelings for him—none at all.

Now Kilburg was looking directly at me. The breeze that had picked up grew stronger, sending a tumbleweed bounding past the fort, lifting a plastic produce bag we had left in the dirt. A dust devil spun elegantly and died. I hadn't stopped crying, but I tried not to show it, blinking away the tears. I told him again that I was sorry. One of the tears landed on my forearm, and even though I had felt it fall from my chin, I thought for an instant that after five long months it had begun to rain. But the clouds had already started to separate, exposing the moon and the stars, floating east toward Sunrise Mountain.

Kilburg knuckled his shoulder. He set the flashlight in the dirt and reached for the prosthetic leg, scowling as he pulled the sleeve over his stump and tightened the laces. I'm not sure why, but it occurred to me, for the first time, that he had a potentially critical illness: if it had cost him his leg, I reasoned, it could just as easily cost him his life. I was suddenly convinced that, like my father, Kilburg wouldn't live long.

"I guess I thought we were friends," he said, a note of fear in his voice.

It was late, and I could feel that I was still pretty high. I didn't know what to tell him. I was tired and I wanted to go home. Finally I stood, brushing dirt from my shorts, and offered Kilburg my hand.

"We are," I said, because a lie seemed less hurtful than the truth.

Longing to Love You

ALL AFTERNOON HE THOUGHT OF HER, EAGERLY IMAGINING the details of her body: her height, her weight, the color of her skin, the curves of her legs, hips, breasts. Now, as Nick walks west through the Tenderloin, nearing the corner of Taylor and Eddy, he feels a prick of anxiety at the back of his throat. Brief but dispiriting—always causing him to second-guess himself—it's a familiar sign that he's doing something he knows is questionable. A cool breeze picks up, heralding the coming autumn, but Nick feels sweat surface on his forehead. He's unsure if he should turn back or carry on. Each building he passes is a liquor store or a laundromat or a bedraggled old flophouse with a neon Vacancy sign. He hurries by them, late to meet My-Duyen, the Vietnamese masseuse he telephoned by way of the yellow pages, a call girl who refers to herself as the "Asian Sensation."

The address is 155 Golden Gate Avenue, between Leavenworth and Jones. When he spoke to her earlier today, she told him to call her from the curbside pay phone at a quarter past eleven. "Generous men only," she said, as if he weren't aware that her repertoire extended beyond the domain of benign, legal massage. "Full service," she added. He stared at her photoless ad in the fluorescent light of his kitchen. "I'm Jack," he told her, giving her his father's name, whispering into the receiver as though someone were around to hear him. "My-Duyen," she replied. She mewled and moaned. When he asked her what her name meant, if anything at all, she paused before answering. "Beautiful," she said, and Nick hoped the name was appropriate.

At the pay phone, he digs a scrap of paper from his back pocket, dials the number he copied from the telephone book. The building is a handsome brick Edwardian with a big stone portico—the kind of building normally found in the Western Addition or Pacific Heights—out of place in the Tenderloin, as though it's lost or slumming. The block is alive with people walking in twos and threes, loitering in doorways, slinking in and out of a corner bar down the street whose windows have been painted black. After several rings, My-Duyen picks up. "You're late," she says. It's eleven-twenty-five. "Second floor, apartment seven. I'll buzz you in."

Ascending the stairs, he finds it difficult to lift his feet, his legs solid with apprehension, and the climb to the second floor seems to take an eternity. For all his unease, Nick is shuddering with excitement, hardly able to believe that he's finally going to lose his virginity. At twenty-three, he considers himself a misfit—an anomaly. Most people spend their college years partying, having sex. Nick spent his reading books in the university library, or else playing *Tetris*, or *The Legend of Zelda*, or *Dragon Warrior*, adrift in the fictive worlds of novels and video games. He reads less these days but plays Nintendo more than ever, an hour or two every night. Of his small group of friends, he's the sole virgin, a word he repeats so often in his mind that it sometimes bears no meaning, the two syllables bouncing hollowly off the walls of his consciousness, morphing into other, similar-sounding words: *burgeon*, *sturgeon*, *Virginia*. It's a Saturday, and most of the people he knows are out on dates, spending time with boyfriends and girlfriends. Nick himself has had only one girlfriend—the German exchange student he took to his high-school prom, a thick-ankled Protestant who was saving herself for marriage—and despite his every attempt to negotiate at least a one-night stand, he wakes each morning alone. That he's resolved to pay for sex only magnifies his long-established feelings of inadequacy and self-loathing.

The door is ajar, a black number seven hanging upside down above the peephole. He steps into the apartment, clears his throat.

"Close it behind you," My-Duyen says, drawing curtains across a giant bay window. Music is playing softly on a stereo, a jazz composition he doesn't recognize. She turns to face him. "You must be Jack."

He left home after high school, vowing never to return, not even to visit. Growing up in Las Vegas, he used to envision the day he would board a plane as an adult and fly off to some better city, escaping forever that place of false hopes and ever-changing luck—a place with more churches per capita than any other city in the United States and a suicide rate twice the national average. During Nick's first semesters at USC those two statistics would interlace in his mind, relevant in some way to his newfound freedom. He moved to San Francisco a little over a year ago, after graduating with a degree in comparative literature, and has decided that no place is without the potential to let you down.

His apartment, a small studio, is on the top floor of an old white-brick building that overlooks the Powell Street cable-car line, a twenty-minute walk from the converted carriage house in Cow Hollow where he works as a copy editor for a weekly trade magazine called *Footwear Today*. Every so often he has a beer or two at Salty's, a seafood restaurant around the corner from his apartment building. Down the hall from the dining area, the restaurant's bar stands at the back of a large wood-paneled room that's always darkly lit, its low ceiling supported by four rectangular pillars that make you feel as though you're sitting below a pier. The walls are hung with fishnets, anchors, and oars, with mounted marlin and tarnished brass astrolabes, and at the end of the bar a model lighthouse stands beside an aquarium that showcases an assortment of sad-looking lobsters, piled against the foggy glass. He likes the kitschy maritime atmosphere, and has taken an interest in the new bartender there, Annie Peterson. She's blonde and tan, and her face glows in a corner of Nick's mind (big blue eyes, a full-lipped mouth, a tiny knob of a nose), hurtling to the fore like a shooting star when he least expects it. Though he's only known her a short time—two, three months—he thinks he might love her.

The other night, Nick was sipping a Redhook when Annie asked him, "What happens if you're in a car going the speed of light and you turn the headlights on?"

"No idea," he said, and shrugged.

"Stumped again," Annie said, slicing lemon wedges on a plastic cutting board. She wore faded blue jeans and a white oxford shirt, her shoulder-length hair sticking out from beneath a purple wool beret. It was eleven o'clock, and Salty's had emptied out for the night. Roy Orbison sang "Blue Bayou" on the jukebox.

"Lay another one on me," he told her. "Scramble my brain."

Annie looked up at the ceiling, set the knife down on the cutting board. "Let me see," she said. "Let me think."

She has a fondness for paradoxical questions—owns a small book of them that she keeps beneath the bar—and Nick finds it both puerile and endearing that she's committed so many to memory. She never tires of watching him labor to assemble a response, narrowing her eyes, placing a slender finger to her lips. Annie's favorite question of all time: *Can a person drown in the Fountain of Eternal Life?* Her second favorite: *Can God create an object so heavy that even He is unable to lift it?* Nick likes obliging her with his earnest attempts at reason, though as often as not he capitulates with a shrug.

"I think I've already asked you all the ones I know," she said, then reached down and pulled the book out from under the bar: *Persistently Pesky Paradoxes.*

"That alliterative title might have you thinking it's a book of tongue twisters," he said, trying to sound smart—trying to impress her—but Annie said nothing in return. She closed her eyes, opened the book to a spot somewhere near the middle. "Bop-bop-bop," she said, scanning a page. "Here's one. 'In order to travel a certain distance, a moving object must travel half that distance. But before it can travel half the distance, it must travel one-fourth the distance, et cetera, et cetera. The sequence never ends. It seems, therefore, that the original distance cannot be traveled. How, then, is motion possible?'"

"That's an oldie," Nick said, finishing off his beer. "Even I've heard that one before. Where'd you get that book, anyway?"

"Ricky gave it to me. A long time ago, when we first met. It was a gift."

It's been six weeks since Annie broke up with Ricky, a taxi driver and aspiring sculptor of whom nearly everything reminds her: the restaurants and movie theaters they used to frequent as a couple, the big yellow taxis that weave through the crowded city streets, the outdoor sculptures at the Embarcadero and Golden Gate Park. He still gives her gifts, lockets and fountain pens and glass figurines that he leaves wrapped in her mailbox, and several times a week he calls her at home or at work, begging to be taken back. The breakup was a result of Ricky's infidelity: Annie caught him in the act with his best friend's sister. He had given Annie a key to his apartment, and she walked in on them one night after her bartending shift, the two of them half-naked on Ricky's kitchen floor. She still loves him, she's said, and wishes she could forgive him for what he's done. Nick adores the sound of Annie's voice, but when she says her ex-boyfriend's name he always wants to laugh. "Rick," "Richard," even "Dick" he could accept. But a grown man who goes by "Ricky"?

"You know what I think?" said Nick.

"I'm afraid I don't." Annie closed the book, replacing it beneath the bar.

"I think I'm going to write Ricky a letter."

My-Duyen is indeed beautiful, with bright green eyes and tea-dark skin and the muscular calves of a bicyclist, her hair shaped in a wedge. She wears a red knee-length dress, open at the neck, and stands bare-foot on the wooden floor. The apartment, a studio not much larger than his, reminds Nick of a chapel: low-burning candles on every surface, the walls aglow with the solemn guttering of a dozen tiny flames. There's a couch, a coffee table, a bookcase, a full-size bed. On a nightstand four wrapped condoms are stacked like casino chips beside a roll of toilet paper. My-Duyen takes his wrist and leads him to the bed.

"Sorry I was so short about being late," she says. "It's just that I have a schedule to keep, appointments all night long."

She's thirty or so, not young but not old either. *Mature*, he thinks, like a friend's big sister. Nick is unable to take his eyes off her, and feels lecherous and rude staring the way he is. He can't quite say what it is that draws him to them, but a shiver passes through him when-ever he encounters a woman of Asian descent. Chinese, Japanese, Filipino, Korean, Thai, Vietnamese—the particular origins make no difference. An irrepressible hunger comes over him, and he can think of nothing but sex. He sees them in Chinatown and Union Square, young Asian women with sleek black hair and soft-looking skin—sees them jogging up and down Powell, hard-bodied and sweating in tight T-shirts and high-cut shorts, their wiry legs bowed like paren-theses. Nick often pictures these women when he masturbates, and he's spent a small fortune at the new sushi restaurant in Cow Hol-low, where he's taken countless lunches simply to eat in the company of the all-female Japanese waitstaff. Now, looking at My-Duyen, he forces a smile to calm himself, the shiver lingering in his limbs like the aftereffect of an electrical shock.

"I would've been here on time," he says, "but I got a call on my way out the door." He doesn't want to admit that he was playing *Dr. Mario*, only moments away from reaching the coveted twentieth level, when he realized the hour. He doesn't want to say that as much as he looked forward to meeting her, he was on an unprecedented roll and thought for a split second about standing her up, staying home and seeing how much farther he could get. "I walked here as fast as I could."

"I don't serve alcohol, but I can get you a soda if you'd like."

"No, thanks," Nick says, folding his hands over his lap to hide his arousal. Sitting beside her at the edge of the bed, he can smell her citrus-scented perfume, a trace of mint on her breath.

"Well then," she says. "Before we get started, I think you have something for me."

Over the telephone she never specified an amount, and so Nick brought only what he could afford, a hundred dollars. He hands My-Duyen the money—three tens, four fives, a fifty—and she counts it out, nodding amicably.

"This'll do," she tells him, and places the folded bills into the nightstand's drawer. "Now we can relax." She scoots closer to him, caresses his arm with the tip of her finger. "What is it you came here for?" she says.

"How do you mean?"

She gives him a slow, off-balance smile. "What would you like to do to me, Jack? What would you like me to do to you?"

"A letter of what kind?" Annie said, palming the lemon wedges into a pile.

"I want to make him jealous," said Nick. "Tell him we're getting married and he isn't invited to the wedding. Tell him we're a thing, you and I, even though we aren't. Generally, I'm not such a vengeful dude, but wouldn't it feel good to make Ricky feel bad?"

Around her, Nick often talks in a manner to which he isn't accustomed—feels more confident, almost cocky, though he can't say why. She's out of his league for sure, but he's never been intimidated by Annie's appearance. Nick knows he isn't handsome, not in any classical sense, but he's reasonably desirable, he's always thought: dark-haired and tall, with a genial, long-toothed smile he's cultivated in adulthood. Every now and then he catches himself wondering what her ex-boyfriend looks like—wondering who Annie finds more attractive, him or Ricky.

"You've never even met him," she said. "He's actually not a terrible person. He just did this one terrible thing. When I think about it, I was really happy with Ricky. Happy in a way I'm not sure I could ever be without him."

Nick and Annie have had dinner together outside of Salty's, have shared nightcaps at nearby bars, though only as friends. Whenever he takes her hand her fingers wiggle free of his grasp, and when he tries to kiss her she turns sharply away. "Not yet," she always says. "It isn't the right time. A new boyfriend's the last thing in the world I need at this point in my life."

In truth, Nick's attempts to hold her hand and to kiss her have been somewhat strained. Despite his feelings for her, he isn't sure he's attracted to Annie—isn't sure his interest in her is carnal. She's an attractive woman by anyone's standards, but she isn't Asian, and there are too many times when he looks at her and feels no shiver throughout his body, no hunger for sex, only a contentment so deep that the second they part Nick longs to be near her again. He's never quite certain, then, if love—*romantic* love—is the right thing to call whatever takes hold of him when he thinks of her, when he's around her. He can make no sense of his preoccupation with Annie, any more than he can make sense of his fixation with Asian women.

Annie took his empty beer bottle, tossed it into a recycling bin behind the bar. "Another Redhook?"

"What's stopping me?"

She got Nick his beer, placed it on the round cardboard coaster that read "Salty's" in big turquoise letters. Then she set to tidying the bar. He watched as she worked through a row of foam-stained pint glasses, plunging each glass into a sink full of soapy water, rinsing it under a faucet, then leaving it to dry on a long white towel. Heady from his third beer of the night, Nick said, "I love watching you move."

Annie rolled her eyes, drying her hands on the tails of her shirt. "I miss the guy," she said, and sighed. "I'm an idiot, but I miss him."

Nick took the coaster from beneath his beer, flicked it back and forth against the tip of his thumb. "Writing utensil, please," he said, and held out his hand.

Annie gave him a pen. He laid the coaster down on the bar, blank side up. *Dear Ricky*, he wrote.

Sex, he wants to say. *I came here to have sex*. But somehow the word seems crass, despite the urgency of his desire and the fact that he's with a call girl. Perhaps because of all the candles, Nick feels as if he's on a date, as if they've reached some decisive juncture that might require him to initiate foreplay. He should know how to act in the presence of such a woman, he thinks: he is, after all, from Las Vegas. But as a teenager he could never bring himself to solicit a prostitute, no matter how much he wanted to, no matter how many of them he would see walking the streets downtown. He wonders what about him has changed, how it was that he picked up the telephone earlier today and dialed this stranger's number. "Are there options?" Nick asks. "Is it up to me what we do?"

"You're the customer," My-Duyen says.

"I guess I'm not sure how we're supposed to begin here."

"Let's try a different angle. What are you into?"

"Anything, I suppose. I mean, within reason."

My-Duyen laughs, as though his answer were the punch line of a joke. She rests a hand on the small of his back. "How about this. You undress and get under the covers, and I'll take it from there. We'll skip the massage, OK?"

"Yeah," Nick says. "Good." He never expected a massage, and finds it unusual that she maintains the pretext of her yellow-pages ad. He takes off his clothes and slides into the bed, watching as My-Duyen shimmies out of her dress. Naked before him, she pulls the comforter down to his knees, the sheet domed over his crotch. Then she pulls the sheet down too, and his swollen penis is exposed. It looks bruised, as if it's been slapped around or stepped on, the shaft a rash-like red, the head darkened to a purplish hue.

My-Duyen's breasts hang sublimely from her body. Between her thighs is a vertical strip of pubic hair, the skin shaved clean around it. She lies down next to him, her leg brushing his, and suddenly Nick feels as if his insides are being liquified in a blender. It's the same way he's felt roaming the aisles at Big Al's, an adult bookstore on Broadway, where he goes several times a week to flip through the pages of *Orient XXXpress* or *Kung Pao Pussy* or *Filipino Fuck*, surveying the glossy images before rushing to the Burger King across the street, slipping into the men's room, and masturbating in a stall defaced by graffiti and glory holes, sometimes evacuating his bowels just after he comes.

"Asian Sensation," he says, the words tumbling accidentally from his mouth.

"What?"

"That's what you called yourself. Over the phone."

"Oh, right." She props herself on an elbow, flattens her hand across his stomach in a tender sort of way. Looking down at his erection, she seems to think for a moment, then says, "Tell me you love me, Jack."

"I'm sorry?"

"Just say it." Her voice quivers. She lowers her face. "For me."

What reason could she have for asking him to say such a thing? Is she putting on some kind of act, he wonders, a show of emotion meant to heighten his excitement? "I'm not sure I understand," Nick says.

She still isn't looking at him. "Three simple words," she says, nuzzling up to him like a cat, curling her warm body into the crook of his arm.

"It's my first time," he tells her, trying to change the subject, though he isn't sure why he's chosen this, of all things, to say. Under normal circumstances he keeps his virginity a secret, hiding it from the world as he might some sordid deed from his past. "I'm a virgin," he says.

"I figured as much. It's nothing to be ashamed of." She reaches down and takes hold of his erection. "Pretend I'm your girlfriend and we do it all the time. Pretend you're going to fuck me," My-Duyen says, "because you love me."

Nick's heart leaps. His lust for her sharpens to a point, and he feels another prick of anxiety at the back of his throat. He's been getting it since childhood, this tiny remonstrative prick, anytime his actions have threatened to further diminish his self-regard.

"Please," she says. "It's a thing I have." She kisses his chest now, once, twice, three times. He can feel himself bulging in her hand, conforming to it. "I need you to say it."

"OK," he whispers, trying his best to keep from coming. "I love you."

He stayed until the restaurant closed, then walked Annie home to her apartment in North Beach, fifteen blocks away. In Nick's back pocket was the short letter he had written to Ricky, the coaster creased into a half-moon beneath his billfold.

"Why don't you come up," she said as they approached her building. She shrugged her shoulders, a breeze riffling the ends of her hair. "It's only eleven. I could use a glass of wine."

"Great," said Nick, excited by the invitation: Annie had never asked him up to her apartment before.

It was warm and spacious, a one-bedroom with high ceilings and a recessed balcony. Against one of the walls stood what appeared to be an arts-and-crafts project of some sort. Two yellow pipe cleaners sprouted like antennae from a white Styrofoam ball the size of a desktop globe. As on a tee, the ball sat atop a Quaker Oats container that rose like a little silo from the inside of an orange Nike shoe box.

"*Mi casa*," Annie said with a sweep of her hand. She took off her hat, her coat, hung them on a hook beside the door. "Welcome."

"Nice place."

"Rent control and tips," she said. "How else could I survive in this city?"

Nick nodded at the arts-and-crafts project. "Interesting furniture."

"Ricky's first sculpture. 'Evolution,' he calls it." She clicked her tongue. "I've been meaning to get rid of that thing for a while now."

Nick had always assumed that Ricky's medium was either plaster or ceramic, not cardboard or Styrofoam. He looked the sculpture up and down, tapping his chin. Then their eyes met and they both broke into laughter.

"Fine," Annie said. "So he's not the *best* sculptor in the world."

She opened a bottle of merlot, poured them each a glass as they settled in next to one another on her small leather couch. The cushions were dry as saddles, faded to a light coffee-brown, and creaked whenever he made the slightest adjustment of his legs. They were talking about the letter to Ricky when Nick noticed the Atari 2600 on the bottom shelf of her television stand.

"Read it to me," she said, nosing the wine. "It was sweet of you to write it."

She had been busy closing up the bar, and Nick hadn't had a chance to show her the letter. But he could tell that he had managed to charm her, that she had taken as some kind of gallantry his juvenile wish to make her ex-boyfriend jealous. He thought about kissing her, which he hadn't tried to do in a couple of weeks. *Not yet*, he imagined Annie saying. *It isn't the right time.* "You're into video games?" he asked, pointing to the Atari.

"Kind of," she said. "I don't know. I bought that thing at a garage sale in Berkeley. It made me nostalgic. They threw in a bunch of cartridges for free."

"Let's play something," Nick said. "What do you have?"

"First the letter. Get it out."

"Only if you promise to send it." He sipped his wine. "I hope I didn't write it in vain."

"We are *not* mailing that coaster to Ricky."

"You haven't even heard what it says yet," he said, and took the coaster from his pocket. He unfolded it, straightened his back against the noisy couch. "'Dear Ricky,'" he began. By the time he had finished the letter—the gist of which was that Annie and Nick were engaged to be married, that Annie hadn't deserved to be cheated on, and that Ricky would do well to leave her alone—Annie had her head on Nick's shoulder, her arm draped across his leg. She had never been so physically affectionate with him before. Nick waited for some sign of arousal—a tingle in his groin—but he only felt happy. It was a relaxing sort of happiness, a concentrated warmth that trickled into every crevice of his body, like the slow pervasion of heat from a shot of bourbon: what an elderly man might feel for his wife, he imagined, after half a century of marriage, sexual desire replaced by the comfort of long-term commitment. To call such a feeling anything less than love seemed to suggest a limited interpretation of the word.

"What if I start asking people to call me 'Nicky'?" he said, tossing the coaster onto the coffee table. "Actually, my mother calls me that, so who am I to judge?"

She patted his knee. "*Jungle Hunt*," she said, sitting up from the couch. She refilled their glasses, setting the bottle down on the coaster. "How does a little *Jungle Hunt* sound to you?"

"Haven't played it in eons, but I'm sure I can hold my own."

Annie crawled across the carpet to the television stand.

"You shouldn't wear makeup," he told her, watching her thumb through a plastic box of cartridges. A thin layer of foundation coated her cheeks, giving her skin the appearance of fine suede, and her lip gloss made her lips look as though they were wrapped in cellophane. "You're pretty anyway."

"If *that* doesn't sound like a line."

When she spoke, Nick could see the inner workings of her neck, taut vertical cords that seemed to sprout from the small hollow between her collarbones. He looked at the raised scar along the side of her wrist—a lovely imperfection—from the time her younger brother shot her with a Winchester air rifle, the skin around the scar a lightish pink, looking, as he studied it, as if it had been welded together by a tiny blowtorch. "It wasn't a line," he said.

"A word of warning," Annie said, inserting the cartridge into the Atari. "I'm going to win."

She did. First she beat him at *Jungle Hunt*, then at *Asteroids* and *Pole Position*. They drank all the while, polishing off the merlot and moving on to an unopened bottle of Café Rica. The liqueur tasted like burned coffee, but they drank it anyway, and when Annie beat him at *Combat* for the third time in a row—her little blue tank trouncing his red one with an onslaught of guided missiles—she leaned over and kissed him, her lips lingering against his for the better part of a minute.

"Where'd that come from?" he said. He was drunk, and he was sure Annie was too.

Annie smiled. "Let me ask you something," she said. "Is there an exception to the rule that there's an exception to every rule?"

"Ready?" My-Duyen asks, beneath him now, her arms and legs wrapped so tightly around him it's as if she's trying to pull him in whole, trying to force his entire body up into what he imagines as the warm, thick jelly of her vagina. But just as he's about to enter her, Nick frees himself and says, "No. No, no, no."

He can't put Annie out of his mind. After their kiss the other night, he stood up from the couch and smiled, telling her it was late and he had to get going, deciding that Annie's drunken advance had in some way cheapened their relationship, whatever it was. But he felt, as he stepped out her door, that the kiss had nonetheless meant something, and during the walk back to his neighborhood he knew that leaving had been a mistake. He feels a sudden allegiance to Annie, as though enlisting the services of a call girl has constituted a betrayal. It occurs to him that My-Duyen is the only person, barring his parents and maybe his grandparents, to whom he has ever said "I love you." He didn't mean it, of course, and yet somehow he spoke the words.

"Why did you need me to say that to you?" he asks.

My-Duyen watches silently as he dresses. After a moment, she says, "It makes it easier. That's all."

A regretful sadness sweeps over him. "I'm sorry," he says, sighing, zipping his pants. "You can keep the money, but I have to go."

Outside, the block is quiet and still. The people have vanished, and the sidewalks lie empty beneath the high stuccoed buildings. He starts north up Jones, walking briskly at first, then speeding up to a run. He crosses O'Farrell and Geary, Bush and Pine, turning right onto California Street. As he passes Grace Cathedral, the Pacific-Union Club, The Fairmont, Nick feels fast and free, keenly alive, dashing through the sleeping city under a moonless sky set with stars.

By the time he's reached Annie's street, his knees are burning, his arms pumping like pistons. At her building, he presses his finger to the buzzer marked "Peterson," bending over to catch his breath.

"Yes? Hello?" Her voice through the little round speaker sounds high and staticky, as if from an amateur radio station.

"It's Nick," he says, then adds awkwardly, "Nick Danze."

"Oh, hey there." A pause. "Come on in."

He yanks open the door, bounds up the four flights of stairs, skipping every other step. Annie is standing barefoot in the hallway in loose-fitting pajamas, pink flannel ones with a frayed drawstring that hangs to her knees.

"Sorry," he says, stepping past her into the apartment. "I know it's late."

"I just got home from work." She narrows her eyes. "You're sweating."

"This won't take a minute," Nick tells her.

He picks up the sculpture, the parts of which are held together by what appears to be rubber cement hardened into beads along the rim of the Quaker Oats container. He carries it out to the balcony, closes the sliding glass door behind him. The sculpture is nearly weightless, and Nick lifts it high over his head, looking down to make sure the sidewalk four stories below is clear of pedestrians. He glances back through the door, Annie watching him with a bemused look on her face from the other side of the glass. Then he sends Ricky's sculpture over the railing.

The parts remain attached during the brief moments of its descent. It floats downward, sailing gracefully through the pale domed light of a streetlamp. The impact is anticlimactic—quiet enough that he knows he hasn't woken any of the neighbors. Nevertheless, the sculpture breaks apart, the shoe box skidding into the gutter, the Quaker Oats container bouncing a couple of times before settling into an expansion joint in the sidewalk, the styrofoam ball rolling lopsidedly down the street, coming to rest against the rear tire of a pickup.

Back inside, Nick takes Annie's hands in his.

"What did you do that for?" she says.

"I'd like to kiss you again," he says. "Would that be OK?"

Annie nods, and Nick leans in, eyes half-closed. Her mouth opens like a choirgirl's, and so he opens his as well. As their faces meet, he feels a combination of fear and disbelief, as though he's hanging upside down in a roller-coaster car stalled at the crown of a loop: as though he's kissing her not for the second time but for the very first. The kiss, with its sloppy excess of tongue, makes him feel like a character in a daytime soap opera. No sooner does he wonder if Annie is enjoying it as much as he is than she tugs at the zipper of his pants and begins to guide him toward the bedroom.

The sex is slow, deliberate, except that Nick keeps slipping out of her, unable to control the spasmodic movements of his pelvis. When he does succeed at remaining inside, the sensation is otherworldly and intoxicating. He lasts longer than he's ever imagined he would, coming in a few tentative thrusts, then collapsing onto his back.

He stares wide-eyed at the ceiling as though he's witnessed a miracle. That he's no longer a virgin is a bizarre and inconceivable fact. Annie lies huddled beside him, making a purling sound with her throat. She kisses his neck, draws a finger down the side of his face. In his mind, he sees them together at the altar of a church, then in a house with a big backyard, then in a minivan driving children to a piano recital or a soccer game. He wants to love her for real, not in some lukewarm, platonic way—wants to *want* her. As they made love, though, he couldn't keep from picturing My-Duyen, and even now his thoughts drift back to her.

He considers admitting to Annie that she's the only woman he's ever been with. Instead, out of guilt for what he's done—or for what he almost did—he decides to tell her about My-Duyen.

"There's something I have to get off my chest," he says, trembling as he runs his fingertips across her shoulder blades, up and down her back. He can feel his pulse beating in his ears. He thinks of Las Vegas, of his journey from that place to this one, from childhood to adulthood, from virgin to whatever he is now. "There's something I need you to hear."

But when Nick opens his mouth again, nothing comes out. He can't form the words. His hand comes to rest on Annie's hip, and she laces her fingers through his. Glancing across the bedroom, he notices the coaster from Salty's, his letter to Ricky, thumbtacked to a bulletin board that hangs above her dresser. He tries a second time to speak, only to discover that he's unable to move his lips, his tongue heavy against his teeth—something holding him in silence, unwilling to let him go.

"Whatever it is," Annie says, "don't say it. Not yet. It isn't the right time."

A Familiar Place

—————————

My MOTHER THINKS I TRIED TO HIT HER DURING AN ARGUMENT we had earlier today, when I confronted her about living beyond her means. She tells me this in the men's department at Dillard's. "I didn't know you had it in you," she says, "to swing at a woman." She maneuvers between the sale racks in a loping stride: she could be a mall walker, a thief, her arms cutting the air as she makes her way through the crowded aisles. I do my best to keep up. She fingers a pair of gabardine trousers, a silk tie, a camel-hair blazer. "Let's get you some dress pants," she says. "The price is right." But she's headed toward the sweaters, stacked plumb beyond the suits and topcoats. She's wrong, of course—I had no intention of hitting her, though I did get so upset that I put my fist through the living-room wall. When I started to cry, she wrapped her arms around me and said, "What you need is a new sweater."

It occurs to me that hurrying through a department store might be my mother's way of inhibiting herself from shopping, as if to linger would only encourage her habit. Not long ago, when she used to spend her free time practicing concertos on the violin, shopping was the sort of thing she considered a nuisance. Only in the three years since my father's death has she been making frequent trips to the mall, to the Forum shops at Caesars Palace, to the outlets at the south end of Las Vegas Boulevard. "Takes your mind off things," she likes to say. The last time I was home I found an American Express statement with a balance of ten thousand dollars bookmarked in a JC Penney catalog.

"You wearing cardigans these days, Nicky?" At the table of sweaters, my mother points to a pea-green cardigan with navy-blue buttons.

"No," I say. "And I didn't even come close to hitting you."

"Note to self: no cardigans."

I'm not a violent person, so when I saw the hole in the living-room wall, a flap of wallboard hanging like a tongue from when I pulled my fist back out, I had the presence of mind to acquiesce. "All right," I said as my mother held me in her arms, both of us winded from yelling. "A new sweater it is." It's my second day home, three days before Thanksgiving, and already we've had two such arguments, earsplitting bouts of cursing and name-calling that have each ended with one of us in tears. It's not so much the shopping I'm worried about but the amount of debt she's managed to accrue, debt my mother has made no effort to repay.

Three or four other shoppers examine the sweaters at arm's length before a clerk gathers them up to be refolded. In the most cordial tone I can muster, careful not to set her off, I say, "Admit it, Mom. You're at it again. How much have you charged?"

"You tried to hit me," she answers with a playful nudge. She shakes an index finger and smiles. "And judging by what you did to the wall, you probably would have blackened my eye or broken my nose." In mock soreness, she thumbs the tip of her aquiline nose, batting her eyelashes in a manner that seems almost coquettish. "I forgive you, of course. You're my child."

In fact, I'm her *only* child, a distinction that meant a boyhood of mollycoddling and scrutiny that lasted into my early twenties, until my father died and my mother turned most of her attention inward. Nowadays it's rare that she's genuinely concerned with anyone's welfare but her own, and I take her desire to buy me something for what it is: a pretense.

"Christ, Mom. Stop being so dramatic. And don't change the subject."

I hate that I lost my temper, that my anger turned destructive, because just last month I tried convincing her to have the walls painted, the carpet cleaned, the overgrown mesquites in the backyard pruned and staked—to make the place more marketable. Since my father's death, she's let it go. I told her she has no need for the two extra bedrooms, for a backyard that used to take me as a teenager half an hour to mow. I told her to sell the place: it's more than she can handle. "Nonsense," she said, and changed the subject.

"We should be at the hardware store buying paint and spackle," I say now, my mother picking through a stack of wool roll-necks. "I suppose you've been smoking, too."

"You'll need a large," she replies.

Outside, rain pummels the roofs of automobiles, a loud, discordant drumming that I can hear through the glass doors that lead to the parking lot. I watch it fall, wondering what my father would think about us, about the distance between us, the turns our lives have taken, the resentment and misapprehension. Not that I haven't asked him. After he died I began writing him secret notes, scribbled onto napkins and Post-its, which I keep dated in a manila envelope. *What have we become?* one reads. *You can't put the toothpaste back in the tube,* reads another, something my father used to say. My mother and I each have our own, tacit ways of not letting go. I was the one who wanted to drive my father's old Buick, lime-green with a rusted grille, to the mall today, but it's my mother who has it washed and vacuumed once a month. I'm as tall and lean as my father was in good health, and when I'm home I sometimes wear his oxford shirts, which hang starched in my mother's closet, or his black wingtips, which she's kept polished to an impossible shine.

She unfolds a cotton V-neck—burgundy, with a thin white stripe across the middle. She fits it against my chest and arms, and it sticks there like a magnet. I tell her I've changed my mind, I have enough sweaters as it is—she gave me two this year for my birthday, both cashmere, from Saks Fifth Avenue—but my mother interrupts, waving her hand in the air like royalty.

"Don't be silly," she says. "Where you live you can never have too many."

"Mom."

"What about yellow?" She runs her fingers up a stack of mustard-colored crewnecks.

"Mother." I peel the V-neck from my chest.

Her eyes jump around in their sockets, revealing a medley of conflicting emotion: affection and outrage, desire and despair. Once a dark chestnut, her irises, it seems, have faded to a cataractous beige. Her clownish smile stretches the long lines of tension in her cheeks.

"What is it?" she asks.

"Let's go home."

I'm scheduled to return to San Francisco after the holiday, but because my mother and I haven't been getting along, I'm considering changing my ticket, eating the service charge and flying back a couple of days early.

"Don't you ever think about moving back here?" she says in the car, her smile sinking into a frown. Whenever I come home, my mother starts asking questions, anxious to solve the mystery of why

I live four hundred miles away. What is it I'm looking for out there? What is it about Las Vegas I don't like? What is it about her?

"I'm happy where I live, Mom. You know that."

We pass a long row of houses, differentiated only by the pastel shades of their stucco exteriors. Red Spanish tile covers the roofs, and the desert-landscaped yards are tame reproductions of the surrounding Mojave. My mother's house—the house in which I grew up—is no exception. I ease my father's Buick over the lip of the driveway. In the backseat is a Dillard's shopping bag containing the burgundy V-neck, for which my mother paid cash. As we scudded through the parking lot at the mall, hunched beneath our umbrellas in the violent rain, I shoved two twenties into her purse to cover the cost.

"As usual," she sighs, "I'll be all alone when you leave." She digs a pack of Marlboros from her purse, tapping one out and sliding it behind her ear like a greaser. She begins humming the first movement of Mozart's "Violin Concerto No. 3," something she played often when I was a child, the muffled notes resonating through the hollow walls of my bedroom. My grandfather had a bow in my mother's hand when she was five years old, and before she married my father she had dreams of becoming a concert musician. By the time I was born she had settled for practicing nights and weekends in the spare bedroom.

"I knew it," I say. "Cigarettes."

When my father died, my mother took up smoking at the age of fifty-one. Two months after the burial she spent half the life-insurance settlement—about forty thousand dollars, more money than she makes in a year working the front desk at a west-side law firm—on a new Mercedes-Benz. "I had to have it," she said, her voice shaky, bewildered, as if the ghost of my father had escorted her to the dealership. She cut off most of her hair, a flat black panel that fell silky and wide to the center of her spine, and colored what was left of it a brownish blonde. Now, with her lined cheeks pouchy like a chipmunk's, my mother looks like Liza Minnelli with a bad dye job.

By March she had sold her violin, a Stentor my grandfather gave her when she graduated high school, and started shopping.

My mother walks briskly past the hole in the living-room wall and into the kitchen. She takes the cigarette from behind her ear, opens the back door, and steps outside for her smoke. A desert squall, the rain has ended, the sky has all but cleared, and from the kitchen, through the open door, I can see the sun melting like a scoop of orange sherbet into stratus clouds behind Mount Charleston, casting a gauzy light over a line of golden-barrel cacti in the backyard. The light filters through the naked branches of the two mesquites that grow wild over the wooden fence. The leaves of an acacia tree drip rainwater onto a bundle of white snapdragons, the water trickling through deep runnels in the soil. In some strange way my mother, pinching her cigarette like a joint, appears as though she's in control of it all, orchestrating the setting of the sun and the dripping and trickling of the rainwater, until an eighteen-wheeler races by on the other side of the fence, its horn blowing a low, deafening honk that causes my mother to start. It's been a long time since she's appeared in control of anything, and for a second I'm not sure what matters more to me, my mother's well-being or my own.

Ralph Lauren hand towels hang in the bathroom, the evidence of her excess, their thick terry cloth plush like velvet. A large-screen television and a sectional take up most of the living room, and a Howard Miller grandfather clock ticks away down the hall. As I did yesterday when I arrived, I wander in and out of doorways as if I'm casing the place, inspecting the items that fill my mother's home, looking for things I might have missed. On the bureau in her bedroom is a women's Rolex, the burnished gold of its band glittering in the lamplight. A mink coat hangs in the closet, and a big down comforter with a flower-print duvet covers the queen-size bed she and my father once shared.

When I return to the kitchen, my mother is slicing vegetables. I take a seat at one of the beechwood barstools she bought at Pottery Barn before my last trip home. There's no bar in my mother's kitchen, and the two stools stand forgotten beside the refrigerator in a way that seems shameful to me, as though they're being punished.

"You'll never be content like this," I say. She shakes her head but makes no reply. "What can I do, Mom?"

"You can hand me the carrots," she says doggedly. "In the refrigerator. I thought I'd make a stew for dinner. Something warm for the weather." My mother is always cold. She refrains from running the air conditioner even in the middle of August, when in an average year the temperature can soar to a hundred and fifteen degrees. Today it's seventy. "It's so chilly outside."

"Let me tell you something—"

"The carrots, Nicky."

"Just listen to me," I say, slowly and in a voice that sounds resigned. "Pay attention for a second."

"I'm your mother, Nicholas!" She brings her fist down on the cutting board, flattening a thick crescent of onion. "Goddamn," she hisses, her voice suffused with what sounds more like regret than rage. In her other hand she grips the knife, her wrist trembling as she looks intently out the window above the sink, past a framed photograph of my father that rests on the sill. "Damn you," she says, feeling like someone else, I imagine, detached from a life that was once her own. When she turns, tears well up in her eyes, spill down her cheeks and onto her blouse. A blue vein worms its way down the center of her forehead. She lowers her face, gulping back a sob, and dries her cheeks with her fingers. "God damn you." With the blunt edge of the knife, my mother sweeps the pile of onion slices into the garbage disposer.

"Look," I say. "I'll order a pizza."

◄◄-►-►►

It's almost midnight, and my mother is asleep. Wide-awake, my thoughts spinning in my head, I make a small pot of coffee, the house creaking and shifting in the wind. I wander around a third time, running my palms over the towels in the bathroom, flattening the soft fabric between my fingertips. Restlessly, I turn on the television and flip through the channels for a bit. I think of the Rolex on the bureau in my mother's bedroom, imagining how it might feel to smash it with a hammer or toss it out the window of my father's Buick into Lake Mead.

In the kitchen, I sip coffee and write my father a note on the back of a grocery receipt: *Greetings from below*. Wind gusts against the windowpanes, piping around the mesquites in the backyard. Earlier in the evening, as we ate our pizza in near silence, more rain began to fall. Now the heavy drops pound the roof in gradual waves, as if sprayed by a crop duster. In the note, I mention the hole in the living room; in vain, I ask for my father's advice.

During the weeks before his death, his stooped shoulders rose and fell with each of his ponderous breaths, taken with the assistance of the oxygen tank he strapped to his back like a scuba diver. White blood cells had ravaged the alveoli in both his lungs. The photograph above the sink, black-and-white and mapped with wrinkles, shows my father thirty years earlier, at the age of twenty-four—my age—a man with a future. He's leaning on a walking stick at the edge of a forest trail, an optimistic smile on his smooth, youthful face.

My father loved the outdoors, and at first his illness didn't hinder our Saturday-morning hikes in Red Rock Canyon, twenty miles west of Las Vegas. We packed sun visors, granola bars, a trail guide published by the Bureau of Land Management, my father's big Yukon binoculars, his canteen, his Swiss Army knife. Along the trails I whittled sticks while my father named flora and fauna. He stopped to pluck berries from juniper trees, pointed out horned toads as they darted into their holes, all the while instilling in me an appreciation for the vast desert that confined our city. "Pinyon pine," he might say, a man who enjoyed studying field guides when he had the time. "Creosote. Manzanita." Early wrinkles crisscrossed his rawboned face, and his front teeth, crooked and flaxen, often caught his lower lip when he spoke. He had silver hair and gold-blue eyes. Tortoiseshell eyeglasses slid to the very tip of his upturned nose. Gazing into the sky, he might hand me the binoculars and say, "Osprey, Nicky, up above." He huffed and he coughed, but he trudged on. I was twelve, thirteen years old, and I wanted to be just like him someday.

The next morning my mother announces that she's going in to work. She took the week off, but there's something she forgot to wrap up on Friday. Because she answers a telephone all day, I can't imagine what that something might be, and I suspect she's on her way to the mall.

I'm not sure what to do with myself in her absence. I write my father another note, this time on the inside of a coffee filter from the box I left out last night: *What is it you're looking for out there? What is it about Las Vegas you don't like?*

I consider patching up the hole, tending to the mesquites out back. Instead, I call Carter, an old friend from the neighborhood—a thing I've been meaning to do. It's been a long time since we've had anything in common, but when my father died Carter flew home for the burial and then called me every week for several months. We've managed to fall out of touch since then, and I invite him hiking in hopes of rekindling a friendship I still value.

We drive up to Red Rock in my father's Buick. Carter, too, is home for Thanksgiving, back from Los Angeles, where he plays bass in a Bob Dylan cover band, Positively 4th Street. During high school Carter and I would come up here late at night to smoke weed and listen to the Grateful Dead. We rolled the Buick's windows down while "St. Stephen" or "Uncle John's Band" filled the high mountain air, heavy and warm in the summer months but otherwise breezy, cool. Sooner or later we climbed up onto the roof, where, young and stoned, we lay back and raised our arms into the night sky like antennae, wiggling our fingers at the stars that hung in a bright multitude over the desert.

It's unseasonably warm today, almost ninety degrees. Mountains of Aztec sandstone sweep the horizon, and the hood of the Buick is aimed long and flat at the narrowing road. In my hands the steering wheel is big and loose, moving back and forth like the wheel of a ship, the whole car floating up and down on its spongy shocks. Blankets of heat quiver up from the pavement, and hot air blows through the open windows. As we near the end of Charleston Boulevard, where the road funnels into two slender lanes of interstate that wind through the Mojave, Carter says, "We've never driven this during the day, have we?"

"Not with each other." The only other times I've been up to Red Rock during the day have been with my father. It was after he no longer had the lung capacity to hike or even climb stairs that Carter and I started coming up here at night, and as I lay back on the roof of the Buick, something about the sheer number of stars above always made me feel privileged and confused—not alone in the universe but privy to a secret I couldn't quite comprehend, an inscrutable beauty that seemed at odds with the ugly reality of my father's illness.

"I brought a little something along," Carter says. "Just like the old days." He rolls up his window and extracts a glass vial from his sock, yanks his keys from a front pocket of his shorts. "Booger sugar," he says. "Time to party."

"Jesus, man. Not while I'm driving."

"Chill," Carter says. "Go the speed limit." He laughs through his teeth. "Like this shit box could go any faster if it wanted to."

"Just be careful, will you?"

He uncaps the vial, dips the tip of a key into the coke. He brings a little mound to his nose and inhales. "Fuckin' right," he says, clearing a nostril with the side of his thumb. "Yes indeed." He holds out the vial as though he's offering a breath mint. "Here. Try a little."

"Do you not see that I'm behind the wheel of a car?"

"Suit yourself. More for me."

"What happened to weed?" I say.

"Weed," Carter says, slouching in his seat. "I live in L.A. now."

In the parking lot of the ranger station, we lace up our boots and swig some water from my father's canteen. Carter looks goofy, diffident, in his black Dylan T-shirt and his cutoffs, out of place against the rugged backdrop. Though tall and muscly, his biceps stretching the sleeves of his shirt, Carter's the farthest thing from an athlete or an outdoorsman. Tube socks rise slender from his boots until they widen just below his knees, his calves thick as grapefruits. He has a steepled head, and his short brown hair sticks out from his scalp like confetti. "What is it we're here to do again?" he says.

With a pair of carabiners, I clip the canteen and my father's binoculars to the belt loops of my shorts, and we head north on the Keystone Thrust, what used to be my father's favorite trail. It wends its way through a deep cirque, past a thin band of cottonwood trees, and into the mountains. Blonde light slices through the canyon, and low clouds tow shadows across the desert floor. The dusty sandstone, veined with sediment, slopes away in patches of crimson and orange, ocher and white. On either side of the trail are several species of cacti—foxtail, mostly—as well as spreads of brittlebush, all of it giving off a collective scent that, from last night's rainfall, fluctuates between something like damp wool and buttered rum.

Carter tromps ahead. I expect him to launch into some drug-induced rant, but he only says, "So this is it: the great goddamn outdoors." I consider talking to him about my mother, but because it's been a while since I've seen Carter, I'm hesitant to burden him with my troubles. I try to come up with something to ask him, something more substantial than, "How's L.A.?" or, "Seeing anyone?" I settle on "What's new with the band?" though he doesn't answer.

Within a few hundred yards I find a decent walking stick, a little too fat but long and weatherworn, smooth except for the black knot that protrudes like a goiter from the wider of its two ends. I take out my father's Swiss Army knife and shave off two or three loose splinters. The knot makes for a better grip, and as I wrap my fingers around it, digging the other end of the stick into the soft earth, I hear Carter say, "Holy crap." He spins around, pointing into the air, a grin taut across his face. "Check out the wingspan on that thing."

High above us, an escarpment eclipses the sun, a nimbus of bright light shining from its edges, darkening the craggy slope to a silhouette against the brilliant sky. Squinting, I see what looks like a golden eagle glide out from behind it. The eagle stalls mid-arc, its wings indeed spanned wide, and cuts back again like a boomerang. When I reach for the binoculars, something strikes my shin with a snap, like a pebble from a slingshot.

I spot the snake, a sidewinder, as it skitters toward a tangle of needle grass on the other side of the trail. Two hornlike scales bulge over its eyes, and its body, thick and brown, flexes like a muscle. The waves of its movement leave a series of S-shaped markings in the dirt, the sound of its rattle like fat in a skillet.

"Shit," I say in a whisper.

Where the fangs went in, above my sock line, is a small red colon, twin dots of blood around which the skin is already darkening into two purplish halos. I unclip the canteen and pour some water over the wounds, my heart hammering in my chest. I've seen a couple of sidewinders in my life, but I've never been bitten, and I don't recall my father ever telling me how venomous they are, only to stay away from snakes.

Up ahead, Carter's still tracking the eagle, his head tilted in a trance. I call his name, and he turns, walking a few paces toward me. When I point to my leg, his face slackens with worry.

"I've got to get to a hospital," I tell him.

By the time we make it back to the Buick, ten minutes later, a slow, aqueous pulsing has commenced around the wounds, as if hot syrup is being pumped through my veins, and I have to lean into the walking stick for support.

On the interstate, Carter threads the Buick in and out of traffic, nearly skimming the running board of a pickup. "Take it easy," I say, my lower leg tingling now as if it were asleep. I imagine an inklike cloud of venom spreading throughout my body and up around my heart.

The nearest hospital is more than twenty minutes away, but with Carter behind the wheel we make it in ten. In the emergency room, a nurse has me fill out forms—my leg elevated on a magazine table, Carter chewing at the cuticles of his thumbs—until a youngish doctor in a crisp white coat escorts me to an empty triage room. He's short and slender, the coat sagging from his shoulders like a toga. I tell him what happened, and he helps me out of my boots and onto a gurney. He presses a finger against one of the wounds, both of which have swollen to the size of Ping-Pong balls. He studies them closely. "You're sure," he says in a high, ineffectual voice, "about the snake."

I nod.

The doctor peers into my eyes, my nose. "Well," he says. "It doesn't seem to be a dry bite, what with the swelling and the pain." He lifts my T-shirt and applies a stethoscope to my chest. "Let me have you breathe. Deep. Hold it. And out now. Good."

The pulsing has worsened, a seismic beat that runs back and forth between my ankle and my knee.

"The pain shouldn't last long," he tells me, "but you'll probably have some flulike symptoms later on—nausea and headaches, nothing serious. I'll have to give you a couple doses of antivenin, just to be safe."

"All right," I say, a tide of relief moving through me.

But as the doctor scribbles something onto a pad, I grow listless, light-headed, my vision blurring. I lie back on the gurney, the ceiling whirling above me, when a needlelike warmth surges into my extremities and everything goes dark.

I wake in a private room with a television. Beside my gurney, my mother sits cross-legged in a chair, watching the Weather Channel.

"Well, well," she says. "Look who's up. It's a good thing we bought you that sweater. They're expecting a front next week in San Francisco. Hi, sweetheart." She leans in and kisses my cheek, runs a hand through my hair. "You've been asleep for hours." On her wrist, hanging like a bracelet, is the Rolex from her bureau. "The doctor thought it was better if you rested. How do you feel?"

I feel awake, rejuvenated, the way you feel the morning after taking a sleeping pill. The wounds are concealed by a layer of gauze and white medical tape, and there's a slight ache in my thigh where the syringe went in. The pulsing in my leg is barely noticeable. "Good," I say. "I feel good."

"It's a miracle you're alive. I always told you and your father not to hike that silly canyon."

Outside, a full moon has risen. My mother stops in front of the Buick, still parked in a visitors' spot just beyond the entrance.

"Where's Carter?" I ask. "Where's your Mercedes?"

"We'll pick it up on the way. I didn't know how long you'd be out, so I let Carter drive it home." She frowns at my bandaged leg. "Poor guy," she says, and lays a hand on my shoulder. She's right, I should be thankful to be alive—I could have been bitten by a Gila monster, stung by a scorpion—but I can't stop looking at the Rolex.

It's when she takes her hand away, the loose watch sliding back down her forearm to her wrist, that I realize it's the Rolex my father gave her on their twentieth anniversary, ten years ago. It was a lavish gift, for special occasions only, holidays and engagements, but to my father's disapproval my mother wore it all the time. I try to think of something to say, ashamed for assuming she charged it to her credit card, for not recognizing it sooner. I haven't seen it on her since before my father's death, and for the first time in as many years I feel defenseless in my mother's presence, as vulnerable as a child.

"My leg's all right," I tell her. "I'd like to drive, if it's OK with you."

In reply, as if she's read my mind, she winks and walks around to the passenger side of the car.

I steer the Buick out of the parking lot, the tires squealing a little as they catch the pavement. Instead of turning east on Charleston, I turn west, toward Red Rock.

"Where are we going?"

"I have something to show you," I say.

"Show me what?"

"I don't know—nothing. Wait and see."

The whole way there neither of us says a word, as if in contemplation of some shared secret, the lights of the Strip flickering in the rearview mirror, shrinking in our wake. My mother's expression is quizzical in the green glow of the dash, and I get a feeling of desperation, a sudden awareness of time that makes me lean harder on the accelerator.

I park the Buick at the edge of the empty lot, overlooking the Keystone Thrust. I leave the headlights on and roll my window down, the air still smelling musty-sweet, brisk, now, against my skin.

"Why did you take me here?" my mother asks, eyes squinted.

The moon looms bright over the desert, and I can just make out the band of cottonwoods that reaches across the base of the mountains. Bushels of sagebrush dot the landscape, illuminated in the headlights like props on a stage. The limbs of a lone Joshua tree, spiky and thick, are frozen in a shrug. A dark wall of rock, veneered with limestone, drops away in a sudden declension. I can see lines of color in the cliffs, the sandstone weathered with cavities and fissures, carved into phenomenal rock formations that appear balanced by an intricate arrangement of weights and pulleys. Clouds lie flat up above, and in between them are faint sprinklings of stars.

"Foxtail," I say, pointing down to the trail, "there on the left. Over there is some sagebrush, and that funny-looking tree is called a Joshua."

My mother looks out into the canyon, then down at her hands folded in her lap.

"Do you think about him?" I ask.

"I miss your father every day of my life, Nicholas. Every day. Sometimes, when I dream, he gets better and everything's all right. He lives. He lives to be an old and happy man."

In the atmospheric light, a metal sign that maps the trail shimmers like a nickel in the sun: silver, opalescent. I'm in a place I've visited dozens of times before, but I feel years away from anything familiar.

"It's so cold," my mother says, and rubs her arms. "Roll that window up."

"Smell that air," I say. "It's something, isn't it?"

"So it is," she says, sniffing the air.

I reach back and retrieve the V-neck from the Dillard's shopping bag, unfolding it and pulling off the price tag.

"Here," I say. "Put this on."

My mother wriggles into the sweater, the sleeves hanging floppily over her fingertips. Without so much as a glance, she says, "I don't know what it is you want from me."

I don't say anything at first. I turn her words over in my head until they begin to sound routine, like something she's said to me before, like a secret note I might have written to my father. I listen to the sound of insects, a soft, ambient drone, and all of a sudden my stomach feels as if it's being wrung like a wet towel. I take a deep breath and reach down and feel around the wounds, thinking of the sidewinder that bit me, imagining it slithering down the Keystone Thrust, my father's trail of choice, hunting for prey—lizards and kangaroo rats and pocket mice—a hungry serpent, doing what it must to survive.

"All of this was once covered by sand dunes," I say at last, feeling the way I used to when Carter and I would climb up onto the roof of the Buick and raise our arms into the night, privileged and confused.

She looks past me. "A long time ago," she replies.

"That's right," I say. "Before that it was under water. The mountains were formed by reactions—chemical and thermal—that turned the dunes into stone. Centuries of erosion shaped them into what they are today. Dad taught me that."

My mother nods knowingly. She closes her eyes, presses her head against the back of the seat. She begins to hum—another of Mozart's concertos, perhaps—the notes soft and vaguely recognizable.

I switch on the high beams, and everything brightens as if by some minor miracle.

"Take a look," I say.

And she does.

Driving Lessons

CLUB VENUS STOOD SECLUDED AT THE DEAD END OF A GRAVEL
road that wound three miles from the interstate into the gaping darkness of the Mojave Desert. To Nick's surprise, it resembled the stately
two-story homes that populated the Oak Park neighborhood in which
he had lived as a young child. He hadn't been back there in years, but
he remembered that his early-boyhood residence had similar fenes-
tration, that its wood trim was the same defunct, sun-faded brown.
Like this one, the house in Oak Park was made of red brick, with lat-
ticed window boxes, a big oak door, asphalt shingles, a Williamsburg
chimney. It was Christmas Eve, and Club Venus glowed with colorful
holiday lights that stretched the length of its gable roof and framed
its casement windows.

During the long drive from his mother's, as he had held his scribbled directions up to the dim light of the Buick's sun visor, Nick had
guessed that the club's owners had managed to claim and convert an
abandoned building, much like the ones that were always material-
izing, windswept and windowless, along the four-lane interstate that

reached from California to Nevada. He had envisioned strobe lights, a velvet rope, bouncers in black. Now, as he locked the Buick and cut diagonally across the grass, the bitter wind of an unusually cold winter spinning past him, saffron-colored blades crunching underfoot like hay, Nick rolled his eyes at his overactive imagination. It was likely, he thought, that Club Venus only resembled his old house in Illinois in subtle ways.

He paused at the concrete stoop that led up to the door. He had never been to such a club—to a "swing club," as it was called—and that it had turned out to be a house made him wonder if he was in the right place. Left of the yard, where he had nosed his dead father's LeSabre between two SUVs, the desert was a makeshift parking lot: two dozen or more automobiles had been forsaken in the dirt among the sagebrush and the black volcanic rock. The moonlit house, which bore no sign advertising the club's name, gave way to a long row of shriveled geraniums, and a tumbleweed drifted ghostlike past a small cactus garden flanked by two giant elms. Nick had been only eight years old when his father had moved the family west for the new job he had taken at the nuclear test site, out near Indian Springs. Since most of Nick's youth had been spent in Las Vegas, he knew that non-native varieties of grass, flowers, and trees, in the spring and summer months, could thrive in the desert. Still, the whole place looked transplanted, he decided, as if it had been uprooted, yard and all, and set down in the middle of nowhere—though it was somehow quaint and alluring, like a bed-and-breakfast, he thought, or a secret cottage from a fairy tale.

Nick had visited kindred establishments: subterranean bondage bars, Asian hand-job joints, the cathouses on the way to Reno, the sorts of places that comprised what he had come to think of as the tenebrous periphery of society. Over the years, his various fixations had driven him to commit acts of perversion and infidelity—he had been cheating on Annie for some time now—and he considered himself heartless and disturbed. He was twenty-six years old, an adult, but no more serious about his girlfriend of the past two and a half years than he had been about his one girlfriend in high school. He had a close affiliation with guilt but a slumbering sense, he thought, of moral responsibility. Back in San Francisco, Nick had discovered clandestine clubs with salacious names: Close Encounters, Sexplorations, The Playpen. He had seen grown men eagerly submit to being bullied by leather-clad dominatrices who, masked and muscled, humiliated their subjects with theatrical contempt. He had watched naked women slither around stainless-steel poles while at their stilettoed feet men had slid their hands into their pockets and manipulated hidden erections with a slow, hypnotic fervor. He had passed late nights in Chinatown massage parlors where for an extra twenty dollars a full-body rubdown culminated in what was referred to by the young immigrant masseuses as a "happy ending." But the promise of sex still had a way of overwhelming him, and as Nick climbed the steps toward the house—his excitement rising to a pitch that always made him shaky and light-headed, made him think that he might somehow black out—he felt a charge deep within his bones, the same charge, he guessed, an addict felt popping a pill or squeezing off a vein.

The door was answered by a neckless bouncer, dressed not in black, as Nick had envisioned, but in a heather-gray sweat suit and white tennis shoes, who checked his ID and collected a twenty-dollar cover charge. The coat check was attended by a high-breasted woman with a glossy valance of black bangs. Nick handed over his father's blazer, which was plaid and made of warm wool with suede patches over the elbows. In addition to the blazer, he wore the Christmas gifts his mother had given him that evening, a yellow oxford shirt and brown herringbone slacks, fresh from their big blue Brooks Brothers gift boxes. Nick also wore his father's black wingtips, argyle dress socks, and striped purple-and-green necktie, and felt that he looked like a schoolteacher or an imbecile. Earlier, while she had cleared plates from the dinner table, Nick had snuck into his mother's bedroom and removed the blazer, shoes, socks, and tie from the section of her closet reserved for her late husband's things. He had then taken from her bureau drawer the keys to his father's car, and when his mother had gone to bed he had pulled the Buick quietly away from the house and headed for the desert. He knew he looked foolish, though he sported with sentimental dignity the items the man used to wear to church on Sundays or out to dinner with Nick's mother. Socks and ties tended to evade exact sizing, Nick supposed, but the blazer and the shoes fit him as if they were his own.

Beyond the coat check was an enormous living room filled with six velveteen armchairs, three mohair couches, and a long glass coffee table on which an arrangement of multicolored tulips had been fanned out like the tail of a peacock. As he passed through the middle of the room, he saw normal-looking people, tastefully attired, in their forties or fifties, conversing as they might at a dinner party. Then he roamed upstairs, where at the end of a narrow hallway he saw a redhead step long-legged from a bedroom, pulling the door behind her and snagging her heel on the gray shag carpet, tottering forward like an ostrich. She, too, was older, though quite beautiful, dressed in blue: a royal-blue V-neck sweater, a sky-blue skirt that settled just below her knees. She wore pumps and no nylons. Her sweater conformed to a slim upper body, and her skirt fit snugly around her hips. Righting herself, she blushed and said, "Aren't I the graceful one."

"I didn't see a thing," Nick laughed. He pointed toward the closed door at her back. "What goes on in there?"

"Privileged information. Stick around and you might find out."

She winked as she brushed past him, disappearing down the stairs. Nick was shaky again, light-headed, his heart racing in anticipation of what the night might offer. There were three other bedrooms, their doors ajar, and he peered curiously into each of them.

Lowly lit by a single, dangling bulb, they contained only a made bed, a metal folding chair, and a box of tissues on a nightstand. He tried to imagine what sorts of carnal indulgences might still be taking place in the bedroom from which the redhead had emerged. Then he wondered if the owners of the club lived on the premises, if the bedrooms were slept in after everyone left. But the medicine cabinet in the bathroom at the end of the hallway was empty, and the walls, painted burgundy or black, were bereft of photographs or other artwork. It was unlikely, he concluded, that anyone regularly occupied the house. He went back downstairs.

That the guests were older was no surprise. Nick's fixations came and went, and he'd had a recent fondness for middle-aged women. He followed their eyes as he walked the busy streets of downtown San Francisco, and when they passed, hugging their purses to their not-quite-fragile hips, he turned and watched them vanish into the restaurants and bars on Powell Street, into the boutiques and department stores in Union Square. Nick was drawn to women with experience, with the wrinkled jowls and spider-veined calves to substantiate it. He dreamt of the limp flesh that, when they bent forward, bunched like an accordion above their drooping navels, of enlarged labia that, when parted, spread like the pectoral fins of a manta ray. He had come to Club Venus because swing clubs were said to be patronized not just by libertine married couples but by widows and divorcées in search of younger men.

Nick owned an old videotape of *The Graduate* that he had watched so many times he could almost quote the movie from start to finish. In his more prurient moods he masturbated to a nineteen-eighties porno flick called *Aged to Perfection III: Midlife Crisis*, which he kept stashed in the bottom of his sock-and-underwear drawer. But most nights Nick toiled over the novel he had been writing for the past four years, a thing he had begun after college, and when he completed his work early enough he walked down to the seafood restaurant where Annie tended bar—where Nick drank for free—and watched the older waitresses scoot in and out of the barroom in their tight-fitting blue jeans. Other nights he devoted hours to charming the lonely spinsters who hung out at the other bars in his neighborhood. From time to time, alone in his studio apartment, Nick would cry himself to sleep thinking about his betrayals, about his general wretchedness, about Annie, who had always been too tall for him, or too young, or too something, due to the mercurial nature of Nick's fixations.

Nick made his way into the family room, which was half the size of the living room and wallpapered in red velvet. A lanky man with a broad, flat chin adjusted the zebra-print codpiece that covered an opening in his black leather pants. The man was thickly mustached and wore a white mesh T-shirt and red cowboy boots, and he looked like Freddie Mercury. Apart from the lights outside, Club Venus was in apparent denial of the holiday, for instead of Christmas songs, bebop jazz played on the stereo, and a few couples, as if at a high-school prom, shuffled or twisted along the wall. Nick saw a woman in orange fishnet stockings, a pink miniskirt, and a yellow sequined tank top, her breasts swinging like wrecking balls as she danced. He saw a man who wore a black tuxedo and a diamond pinkie ring, and another who was unseasonably attired in a Hawaiian shirt, Bermuda shorts, and flip-flops. Nick examined his own outfit. Had he entered some kind of costume room? He didn't think so. He watched two women in matching silver pantsuits French-kiss next to the stereo.

"Are you aroused?" said a voice.

When he turned, the redhead was standing directly behind him.

"Me?" he said. "Hardly." He shrugged twice, looking away in embarrassment. Across the room a fat man in a love seat exposed himself, the man's sweater hiked up above a walnut-sized navel, his unzipped blue jeans splayed like wings beneath a hairy torus of stomach.

"Indra," said the redhead, extending a freckled hand. Her shake was firm but friendly, her skin soft like brushed cotton. "It's all right that you were watching them. That's allowed here."

"I'm Nick," he said. "Nick Danze. And I was only watching them as a spectacle." She gave him a slow, squinty smile. "I'm more interested in the big guy with his pants undone."

Indra followed his gaze and laughed, a high, happy sound that, despite the crow's-feet at the outer corners of her small green eyes, bespoke something youthful.

"Right," she said. "Of course you are."

Nick rocked back and forth on his heels, pleased with himself for making her laugh, nodding, he thought, like a bobblehead doll.

"I've never seen you before," she said. "You're new here."

"It's my first time. At a place like this, I mean."

Indra narrowed her eyes in a way that suggested he was both a novelty and an asset. She seemed to think for a moment. "A neophyte," she said.

"Yeah," said Nick, "I suppose. You have a pretty name," he said. "What does it mean?"

He had never heard such a name, though the question seemed banal, one that she had most likely been asked a million times before. But Indra obliged, explaining that she had been named after the Vedic god of storms. In Vedic times, she said, Indra had been thought of as a defender of mankind against the forces of evil. Hippies for parents, she confided, the sixties. But she was no younger than forty-five, Nick was sure, which meant that she had probably been born sometime in the late forties.

Indra was recently divorced, and she worked, she said, as an accountant for one of the local casinos, El Cortez. She had come to Club Venus by herself, as she always did. She liked Nick's tie, particularly the way it disagreed with the rest of his outfit—this she divulged with a slight tilt of her head. Her nose was sharp and isosceles, and a fiery ringlet of hair fell across the long hypotenuse of its bridge. Known as the strongest of all the Vedic gods, Indra, she said, had been thought to have the power to revive slain warriors who had fallen in battle. Nick wondered if Indra was her real name.

"It's always nice to meet someone whose name means something," he said. "Mine doesn't mean anything. Boring. American."

"Consider yourself lucky. How do you think I feel? You can imagine the teasing."

"I don't believe it. You're too attractive. I'm sure you were just as good-looking as a kid. The good-looking kids never get teased."

"You're sweet," she said, blushing like she had in the hallway upstairs, "sweet to say so."

Nick felt the beginnings of an erection. He wondered what Indra would sound like in bed. Would she squeal, grunt? Would she scream his name?

"So anything goes here, right?" he said. "What I'm saying is—"

"Relax, sweetie. You're doing just fine."

Nick could feel that he himself was now blushing, and he looked around the room during a long silence. Past Indra he saw the fat man's face lift—the man's perfect semicircle of a chin a smile beneath a smile, his razor-burned neck ballooning like a toad's—as a slender blonde in a gold bustier passed by his love seat, making her way toward Freddie Mercury.

"Well, good," Nick said at last. "Wouldn't want to say the wrong thing and have to face the sweat-suited gladiator at the front door."

Again Indra laughed, dragging a glistening tongue across straight white teeth.

After a time they wandered into the dining room, where an antler chandelier hung low over a cedar picnic table on which had been placed wooden snack bowls, two-liter bottles of soda, and a tower of Styrofoam cups. Over Pepsi and potato chips, Nick told her about life in San Francisco and the plodding effort of his novel. He found himself surrendering the unadorned facts of his existence, not lying or embellishing as he often did with women. But he kept secret that he had a girlfriend, and, considering his surroundings, he wasn't sure why.

"Listen," Indra said. "I don't usually do this, but would you maybe want to go somewhere else? You seem nice, and I've been here for a while already, and I'd really like a drink. That's the problem with this place—no liquor license. It's against my judgment to leave with someone, with a stranger, but like I said you seem . . . I don't know, safe."

"I'm pretty sure that was a compliment."

Indra laughed yet another time, Nick's erection asserting itself against the zipper of his slacks.

"I never got to see what was in that bedroom upstairs," he said.

"Our coats," said Indra, as though she hadn't heard him. She took his hand and ushered him back through the family room, past Freddie Mercury, who for a handful of entranced spectators—among them the fat man, his blue jeans heaped around his ankles as he stroked himself—was now being fellated by the slender blonde in the gold bustier. This was what Nick had come to see, to take part in. He had arrived only an hour ago, but leaving with Indra would of course make his twenty dollars worth it.

Suddenly she stopped.

"I took a cab here," she said. "You have a car, right?"

"Sure," said Nick. "Just outside."

"Good. I don't drive."

Nick warmed his fingers against the vents as they motored through the darkness, winding along the gravel road that led back to the interstate. Indra had removed her pumps and placed her feet up on the dash, her skirt bunched in her lap. From the corner of his eye, in the listless light of a full moon, Nick could see her long, freckled legs, the white skin that stretched flat over the twin hilltops of her knees. In the rearview mirror, through a wake of dust, a jagged line of mountains blotted out a portion of the starless sky. Down below, the tires kicked up stones and grit, the sound of some great machine grinding its contents into a fine powder. Indra stretched her neck taut, flattening her red locks against the headrest.

"My feet," she said. "They're killing me. Damn shoes. You don't mind?"

She pointed to where her heels met the dash, its vinyl cover split and faded from the brutal heat of long desert summers.

"Not at all. I thought we'd head downtown. Fremont Street—vintage Vegas. What do you say?"

"Perfect."

Timidly, Nick reached over and began massaging her left foot, his other hand steadying the wheel. He pulled the foot closer, positioning it in the center of the dash, just above the radio. The skin was clammy like a wet suit. Glancing over, he could just barely see that the tight shoes had left their reddish impressions around her toes, the nails of which were painted navy. They were wonderful toes, thought Nick, bony and callused, weathered with mileage. With his index finger, he probed between them. A heady odor wafted up to his nostrils.

"Sorry," she said. "They stink."

"I don't smell anything," he lied.

With his thumb, he kneaded her almost inflexible arch. Then, with confidence, he ran his fingers around her ankle and lightly pinched her Achilles tendon. He had once had a fixation with feet.

"Wow," said Indra, "you're the best."

Nick listened as she talked of all the interesting people she had met at Club Venus, of how they satisfied both her sexual and social needs. She had made friends there, she said, though Nick couldn't remember her saying good-bye to anyone as they had left the club.

She claimed the regulars formed a kind of community, of which she had begun to consider herself a member. Nick wondered if her community of swinging sex fiends, interesting as they might be, took the place of relatives or real friends. She was gregarious and, he could tell, kind, but he got the impression that she was also a loner.

Nick had seen Club Venus advertised in a free publication called the *Raunch Report*, a weekly paper he picked up from time to time at a local adult bookstore in San Francisco. "The Southwest's Premier Swing Club," the ad had read. He had called the number, long-distance, and spoken to a raspy-voiced woman who told him that, holidays included, the club was open seven days a week until four a.m., that you had to be eighteen to enter, and that, except on "Swingles Night," there was a cover charge for single men. She had then snarled into his ear a concise set of directions to the club. Despite what the woman had said about its days of operation, Nick had been surprised to find Club Venus open—with a sizable crowd in attendance—on Christmas Eve. Didn't they have families, these swingers? Didn't they have anywhere else to be? And what did they do with themselves when they weren't out having sex with one another? Were they gainfully employed? Could one's dentist or auto mechanic be a swinger? Vampires, Nick thought, sinners. But how was he any different? What had *he* been doing at such a place on Christmas Eve? He should have been home, asleep in his old bedroom, but he was glad to be out of the house. Annie had gone home to Los Angeles for the holidays, and Nick had flown in by himself the day before, dreading another Christmas—his fifth—without his father. As the plane had descended over the sandy mountain ranges that wreathed the Las Vegas valley like giant stalagmites of brown sugar, it had dipped low before the runway, skimming the planned developments near McCarran Airport, and Nick had been able to spot his mother's boxy pink house—the one he had lived in as a youth. Stuccoed and, from both the air and the ground, modest-looking, it had sailed by in a winking blue sea of inground swimming pools, not a thing like the custom-built two-story in which he had spent the first years of his life, back in Oak Park, Illinois, two thousand miles away.

Earlier that evening, as she did every Christmas Eve, his mother had played Bing Crosby on the stereo, and the two of them had picked their way through their turkey dinners, then exchanged gifts—a day early, a family tradition, though a somber and meaningless affair without his father. Nick's father had been witty and knowledgeable, a reader of history, a devout Catholic of high moral standards—confident and approachable, like a pilot or a priest—and his attendance had always complemented any gathering. Nick's love for him had bordered on idolization: as a child, he had once dressed as his father for Halloween, borrowing the plastic goggles and yellow hard hat the man had carried with him to work every day. During Nick's high-school and college years, they had shared affection for the Chicago Cubs, Miles Davis, F. Scott Fitzgerald. Nick's distaste for Las Vegas—for its broken promises, its hyped immoderation—had only intensified over the years. What he disliked about it now, though, wasn't just the city itself but the absence of his father from it as well. His father had gotten sick, he had died, and despite the time that had passed, coming home always forced Nick to confront these two painful truths. Christmas had become an agitating formality. A week into December, the man would have shown up with some crazy Douglas fir tied to the roof of his car—too wide for the front door, in need of pruning—and later he would have strung lights along the roof and around the big clay-green mesquite in the front yard. But there was none of that now, no tree, no lights, only the dusty cardboard box in his mother's garage marked "XMAS DECORATIONS." Nick missed his father with a forceful blend of nostalgia, anger, and pain, the way he presumed the dead were usually missed. As an only child, what he missed more, even now as a man, was the intimate security of his little family of four, of homey Christmas mornings with his mother, his father, and his cairn terrier, Kepler, who had also died.

"So," Nick said, "how long have you been going there, to Club Venus?"

Indra had adjusted herself in her seat so that her legs were crossed in his lap, her head propped against the foggy glass of the passenger window. They had reached the interstate, driven it for miles, and exited onto Sahara Avenue. With his free hand, Nick now massaged both her feet, the skin of which remained damp and supple, even though the Buick's heater still huffed warm air into the car.

"Hard to say. Six, nine months, I guess. Not sure, really."

"Six or nine?" he said.

"I'm not sure, Nick," Indra said brusquely. "You don't want the truth anyway. That's not why you picked me up."

A guardedness had crept into her voice since they had left the desert, her expression dour in the green light of the dash, as though she had slowly begun to recognize herself as the butt of an ongoing joke.

"*I* picked *you* up? If I'm not mistaken, it was the other way around."

"Whatever. Doesn't matter. I'm not all that concerned with truth anymore. But the people I've met at Club Venus, they are. They're interesting to me because they don't hide from it. They're real. Unlike us."

Nick firmed up his hold on Indra's feet, clasping them in his hand.

"I don't know. You feel pretty solid by my standards," he said, a Hail Mary of a joke. He let go and pinched the shoulder of his steering arm. "So do I," he said. "Solid matter. Real."

Indra smiled thinly.

"Cabbing it out there must cost a fortune," he said.

"We live in fear, you and I. Am I wrong? We're scared."

Nick didn't know where she was going with this, but he entertained the question anyway: he was no more fearful than anyone else—sick, he thought, selfish, but not fearful.

"That why you don't drive?" he said.

The tip of Indra's tongue peeked from the two polished rows of her teeth.

"Precisely." She nudged her toes into his hand. "My feet are cold," she said dryly.

Nick uncrossed her legs, placing them side by side, and rubbed each foot in a circular pattern. It was hard to tell how serious Indra was, but he found their conversation thrilling.

"All right," he said, making a left onto Las Vegas Boulevard. "I'll bite. Why aren't we real? What is it we're scared of?"

"Teach me," she said.

"How's that?"

"I want you to teach me."

"Teach you what?"

"How to drive."

He stopped rubbing Indra's feet.

"I thought you were afraid," he said.

"I am. I've been afraid all my life, of a lot of things. I was afraid of my husband once—my *ex*-husband, I should say. But he doesn't scare me anymore. He used to drive me to work every morning. There was something nice about that. It was maybe the only nice thing about our marriage. Since we split up I've been taking the bus, impossible in this city. I want to learn to drive a car."

"Well, you could always—"

"Right now," she said peevishly. "I want to learn tonight."

Indra looked as if she were about to throw a tantrum, her arms folded tightly over her chest, her eyes fixed on a point somewhere outside, beyond the bright swath of the Buick's headlights.

"You're serious?"

"Teach me to drive this thing," she said. "Then we'll grab that drink. I'll settle for an abridged lesson."

Nick wondered about her former marriage, whether she had been taken for granted, abused. She was no longer the sociable seductress he had met earlier in the evening, but learning to drive obviously mattered to her—it mattered more, for now at least, than a drink or sex—and in some way he liked her for that.

He was quiet for a long moment.

"OK," he said. "Let's do it."

Up ahead was an Albertsons, and Nick guided the Buick into a spot in its littered parking lot, circumventing stray shopping carts and shattered beer bottles. Outside, the wind stung his face. When they passed each other around the rear of the car, Indra was glowing with what looked like the empty-headed hopefulness of a beginner.

"First things first," he instructed. "Buckle up."

"I'm not a moron," she said. "I just don't know how to operate an automobile."

"Fair enough. But you'll want to lower that."

Nick gestured at the rearview mirror, whose smudged glass was divided into two equal parts by a vertical hairline crack. Indra adjusted the mirror.

"She's twelve years old," said Nick, "but she runs."

He lifted his father's keys, dangling them in front of his face, whiffing their metallic odor in the confined air of the Buick. The smell of keys usually reminded him of licking a nine-volt battery or tasting blood; now it reminded him of the day his father had taught him to drive, more than a decade ago.

"The big one starts her up."

"Again, not a moron."

"Hey," he said, "you're the one who wanted a lesson."

"Correct. So teach me, sweetie."

Nick defined the pedals at Indra's feet, the knobby-ended levers that protruded from either side of the steering column. He spelled out what he considered to be the major rules of the road, the ones he could think of, then told her she would have to back the car out to avoid the concrete parking block that abutted the front tires. She started the Buick—an automatic, he had explained—and shifted it into reverse. Like a seasoned driver, she flung her arm across the passenger headrest to look through the rear window.

"Good," he said. "Always turn around. Never trust the mirror. Now watch for the broken glass when you pull out."

Forty minutes later they were heading north on Las Vegas Boulevard, away from the dome of white light that breathed high above the Strip. Nick made sure they were traveling below the speed limit, but every so often Indra sped up to thirty-five, remaining prudently in the far right lane.

"I never thought it would be so easy," she said, "or feel so good." She pointed her chin toward the road, her expression courageous—triumphant, Nick thought. "I want to drive to France, or Morocco. Let's leave tonight."

"We'll need long bridges for that. You're only using the one foot for the pedals, right?"

"Only the one, sir."

Indra patted Nick's knee, winked.

"Ten and two," he scolded. "No carelessness. This is only your first lesson."

"I'm buying myself a car," she said. "A red one. A convertible."

As they glided through a series of green lights—past striptease clubs and pink motels and drive-through wedding chapels, past tattoo parlors and pawn shops and twenty-four-hour convenience stores fluorescently aglow in the chill Las Vegas night—Nick observed the lack of holiday decoration. Once, as a boy, he had traveled to New

York City with his mother and father during the Christmas season, and he remembered how the leafless trees lining the numbered streets had twinkled with tiny white lights, how the storefront windows had framed elaborate displays of Santas and elves. Here, the streets never seemed to look any different, no matter what the season, and although this ordinarily bothered him, Nick caught himself smiling at the familiarity of his hometown.

"A Corvette," Indra continued, "or a Lamborghini."

Nick coached her through a U-turn, and soon they were back on Sahara, where they came to a red light. The Buick rolled to a smooth stop.

"Nice," he said. "You've got it."

Beyond the light was a ramp that led back to the interstate.

"May I?" said Indra.

"May you what?"

She nodded toward the ramp. "I'm not afraid anymore."

"The highway?" he said. "This is only your first—"

"My first lesson, I know, I got it. I can handle it. I promise."

"I don't think it's a good idea to—"

"Please," she said.

Nick stared hard at the dash, then at Indra. Dreamy-eyed, she clutched the wheel like a racecar driver, her hair, copper-colored in the half-light of the front seat, tucked neatly behind her ear, tumbling to a curly mass at the edge of her shoulder—her ear long and contoured, sleek like the skin of an apple. Nick wanted to give it a kiss, not because he had a thing for ears or apples but because for an instant he imagined loving Indra, marrying her, caring for her as she grew old twenty years his senior.

Nick groaned, scratched at his temple. Outside, a lone streetlamp arched its neck like a sad giraffe, glooming over the dark stretch of asphalt that lay wide open before them. Far off somewhere a motorcycle growled.

"What's the matter," she said, "scared?"

"Like hell I am."

"Well then?"

For the second time that night, Nick heard himself say, "OK. Let's do it."

"Let's drive!"

"You'll stay at the speed limit, though, you hear? And if we hit any traffic, you're done, period. Deal?"

"Deal."

But on the interstate Indra gunned the engine. She opened it up to sixty, sixty-five, leaning hard on the accelerator, her hands at ten o'clock and two o'clock where Nick had said they belonged. Nick watched the orange dial of the speedometer move briskly past the double digits. He watched it vaguely enchanted, pretending he was witnessing something magical: the dial was an hour hand swinging counterclockwise, his father's Buick a time machine programmed to deliver them both to some undisclosed place in history. The dial hovered before approaching seventy. Then seventy-five. Eighty. Nick reached for the armrest of the passenger door. Part of him wanted to move his lips, to protest, but another part of him—a part seduced by the unforeseen, gripped, maybe, by the queer exhilaration of spontaneous detachment—favored silence. Indra piloted the car into the fast lane, which, as far ahead as Nick could see, contained only the Buick. She hugged the bends, overtaking the half a dozen or so automobiles in the adjoining lanes. Nick saw the skin of her knuckles tighten. He saw madness or arousal in the way her upper lip curled toward her nostrils, which flared beneath her intrepid glare.

She took the Buick to eighty-five, ninety. Nick swallowed hard, shut his eyes, feeling the guttural thrum of the six-cylinder engine. Then he found himself thinking odd and unrelated things. He wondered if Annie was awake in Los Angeles, wondered why there were only four seasons, only twenty-six letters in the English alphabet. He thought back to the seventh grade, when he had experienced the first of his numerous fixations, acting on a strange desire to erotically stimulate Kepler, his cairn terrier, who had shook with pleasure as Nick stroked with thumb and forefinger the little dog's slippery red baster of a penis. He thought about his mother, about whether she'd had sex since his father's death, whether she still desired men. He had a sudden awareness of his insignificance in the universe. He wanted to skydive, swim a mile in shark-infested waters. He wondered how many people had died that night, or been born. He wondered if Club Venus vanished every morning at sunrise.

The old car rose and fell on its shocks, the hum of the tires filling him, growing louder inside his head until, soothingly, it diluted his thoughts. Then he heard Indra yell, "Fuck!"

Her leg kicked wildly at the floor of the Buick. He figured she was having a muscle spasm. "What?" he said. He blinked his eyes. "What's going on?"

"I can't feel the brakes. The brakes are gone."

"Don't screw around."

"I'm serious, Nick, they're gone!"

The speedometer read a hundred and five. A tear streamed down Indra's right cheek as she kicked with both feet now at the brake pedal.

"Whoa," said Nick. "OK, calm down. Let's both just stay calm. The highway's dead, and it pretty much keeps on going, so we're not in any trouble yet."

"Christ, Nick!"

Nick cracked his knuckles. He checked that his seat belt was still fastened. He began to chew at the nail of his thumb. With his other arm he braced himself, bridging it securely against the dash. He felt his chest tighten around him, tiny fingers of muscle clenching his bones. A wave of molten panic swelled in his throat: he had let things get out of hand. He pictured a horrible accident, sirens and twisted metal and bright pink flares diverting traffic, then his burial, his widowed mother mourning her only child. He tried to collect his thoughts.

"Whoa," he said a second time.

As if she were extinguishing a small fire, Indra attacked the pedal with heavy feet, rising from her seat a little each time she stomped it. Frantically, she squeezed and shook the wheel.

"Calm the fuck down," Nick said, his voice mousy. "Keep the damn wheel steady. We're going very fast, so try to relax. And whatever you do, don't step on the emergency brake. We'll skid out of control at this speed. You're gonna have to ride this out."

With so few automobiles on the interstate, it was possible that the Buick would simply coast along, gradually slowing down in its long, unoccupied lane before coming to an eventual stop. What little Nick knew about cars he had gathered from a high-school auto-shop class, and he seemed to recall that an interruption of pressure in the master cylinder could cause a car's brakes to fail—sometimes only temporarily, he thought. But he hadn't a clue as to how to handle such a situation, and ahead he could see the interstate sloping left.

"Nick."

"I know," he said. "Just hold on. You can do this."

Then he remembered something his father had told him, something the man had said in passing the day he had given him his first driving lesson. It had been a long time, but it came to him now like a backhand to his skull.

"Pump the brakes," he blurted.

"There *are* no brakes!"

"Try it anyway. Try pumping the pedal instead of slamming on it." His father had said the technique was a way of preventing a car's brakes from locking up on a rain-soaked street, but Nick had never attempted it. His glance fell to Indra's feet, which remained bare. He wanted to reprimand her for driving shoeless, though given their predicament he held his tongue. Her pumps lay overturned on the floor between his legs—somehow he hadn't noticed them earlier, or that she hadn't put them back on before taking the wheel—and for a split second he thought not of impending death but of Indra walking barefoot across the Albertsons parking lot when they had switched seats. It had been strewn with broken glass—she had jeopardized her wonderful toes. "Look," he said. "Does the pedal give at all, even a little, or is it all the way to the floor?"

"It gives, just a little. It's about an inch from the floor, I think."

"I want you to pump it, then. Pump it lightly at first. Just sort of tap it to create more resistance. Can you do that?"

"Yes." Indra's voice crackled. "I'm tapping it," she said, her face screwed up in fright. "I'm tapping it, but it's all loose. Shit."

"Just keep it up, maybe a little harder now. Maybe with a little more pressure. And stop using both feet."

She followed his orders, working the pedal, gauging the movement of her leg, her single-minded effort resulting in nothing. Of its own accord, the car had already slowed to eighty, but outside the ground still rushed by in a maddening blur, the interstate beginning to arc into its long decline.

"It's not working, Nick. The brakes aren't there."

"Keep trying," he commanded. "Keep at it. Take a breath and let's work the problem."

Indra let out a whimper as the Buick approached the oncoming bend. She hugged it as she had the others, but her arms trembled as though she were gripping a small jackhammer, the heavy car gaining momentum. Soon they came to another bend, then another, and she managed to hug these as well, her cheek ruddy with tears that guttered into the corner of her mouth.

"Fucking hell," she said.

Nick saw the two of them sailing off the edge of some cliff like Thelma and Louise. He didn't want to die. He figured he deserved whatever might happen to him, but he wanted badly to live. He imagined tossing open the passenger door and, in a dramatic last-ditch attempt at self-preservation, diving from the Buick at a thousand miles an hour. But in a single, violent jolt, the brakes kicked in, pitching him toward the dash, his seat belt promptly yanking him back.

"Jesus," he said.

The car decelerated all the way to twenty, where Indra held it.

"I think we're OK," she said—prematurely, Nick thought, his fingers plunged into the dash's soft vinyl cover. But he felt the muscles in his chest slacken, and outside the ground moved slowly by.

"I think we're OK," Indra repeated, drying her cheeks with the heel of her palm.

"If scaring the crap out of me was your goal, you succeeded."

"Fuck off," she said in a voice that was almost childish. Remarkably, in shock perhaps, she seemed to be holding back laughter. "Screw you," she said. "It's your piece-of-shit car."

Nick had expected her to pull over right there on the interstate, to hand over the wheel, angry and afraid. The car had been brakeless for at least a couple of minutes, long enough to terrify anybody, especially a new driver intimidated by the road. And Indra had certainly been terrified, all the way to tears. But overall she had held it together, and she now veered confidently across two open lanes into the far right one, aiming the hood of the Buick at an exit that led to Valley View Boulevard.

Nick didn't think he was in shock but he, too, felt giddy. Then Indra unleashed her laughter and together they roared.

When she pulled into a nearby Chevron station, Nick assumed they would switch seats again and head downtown. But Indra called the Buick a death trap, cutting the engine and dropping the keys into Nick's lap. It was late anyway, she said, and she was happy to call it a night. To Nick's astonishment, she was still laughing, shaking her head in playful condemnation while she arranged herself in the driver seat. But there was a tremor in her wrist as she reached down between his legs for her pumps, and Nick watched a late tear spill from her eye.

"I'll flag a cab," she said, shutting the door behind her. "You'd do well to take one yourself." She kicked the Buick's front bumper. "Have this thing towed in the morning."

"I'm good," said Nick. "It was an isolated incident."

"Suit yourself."

"Hey," he said. "You all right?"

"I think so."

"You were great, you know. You did an excellent job back there."

"I'll stick to the bus," she said. "But thanks for the lesson, sweetie."

They were silent during the five long minutes it took for a taxi to arrive. Indra appeared lost in thought, staring meditatively down the quiet boulevard, her arm bent in the air as if signaling a turn. Nick drummed his fingers against his thigh. Impulsively, he said, "What were you thinking, by the way, driving so fast—driving barefoot?"

"I'm off," said Indra, stepping toward a yellow taxi that eased to the curb. "You're a gentleman for waiting with me." She handed him a business card from her purse, looking at him evenly. "Merry Christmas," she said. "Call me. Or don't."

Leaning in, he kissed her good-bye, their tongues touching before Indra backed away.

"I'll see you," she said.

Nick pumped the brake pedal several times as he drove back to his mother's, remaining under thirty. He would tell her to have the brakes fixed, and he would devise a story to explain when he had taken the Buick out and learned of the problem. Tomorrow he might look back and note, with a kind of unhitched curiosity, the recklessness of not leaving the car behind to be towed, as Indra had suggested. But for now he had a fearless trust that he would make it home unharmed. For all he knew, Indra's pumping of the brakes had had nothing to do with what had caused them to return, but Nick wanted to believe that by making that suggestion he had saved their lives. He couldn't help feeling irritated: his trip to Club Venus had been a vain attempt, the entire night a disappointment. At the same time, he felt clever and resourceful, like a survivor.

And yet, minutes later, Nick began to feel sorrowful. A familiar, hovering emptiness descended upon him, and he turned the car around, regardless of its unreliable brakes, and got back on the interstate. He exited onto North Las Vegas Boulevard and drove until he came to the old Woodlawn Cemetery, navigating the Buick through its narrow wrought-iron archway. It had been a year or more since he had visited his father's grave, and he had always come here with his mother, holding her hand as she bowed her head to the earth and prayed. The cemetery was far from her neighborhood, and his father the history buff had requested it as his final resting place only for its historical significance: once the only burial ground in southern Nevada, it dated back nearly one hundred forty years. Floodlights traced the cobbled walkways through the short, dead grass, and even on holidays there stood by the entrance to the big stone mausoleum a uniformed night watchman, who smiled as Nick drove past.

He parked the Buick and made his way down one of the lighted walkways, which meandered into an endless garden of headstones that grew from the soil, crooked and decaying, like rows of neglected teeth. He found his father's plot with ease. The headstone was still new-looking and it was exactly eight rows in (a fact Nick recalled by reminding himself how old he had been when his father had moved the family to Las Vegas), towering a few feet higher than the two half-sunken stones between which it was wedged. The man's name was etched cleanly into the buffed limestone. Nick knelt in the dewy grass. He wasn't religious but he had been raised Catholic, so he made the sign of the cross and placed his hands together. He wasn't sure what to do next. No words came to him, and he felt silly. After a moment he stood, the knees of his new herringbone slacks soaked through to his skin.

Around his neck his father's tie was cinched closely in the Windsor knot the man had taught him for his first communion, and it took some effort to loose it from his collar. Next he took off the blazer, then crouched to remove his father's wingtips and argyle socks. He folded the blazer lengthwise at the foot of the headstone, and over its fuzzy wool he spread the socks and the tie. He placed the shoes neatly on top.

The grass numbed his feet, the stiff blades stabbing upward between his toes. The air blew past his open collar and into his shirt, freezing his chest and his arms. It was past two, Christmas Day, but late as it was, Nick thought about calling Annie when he got back to his mother's. He wanted to tell her that he was in love with her, that he wished to spend the rest of his life with her, though he knew these were lies.

Above him the moon hung round and luminous, a human face, another watchman of the night. He turned toward the car, shivering as he walked barefoot through the rows of headstones. In his throat he felt another wave of panic, hot and tidal, worse than when the Buick's brakes had failed, the landscape seesawing as he faltered across the cold stone underneath his feet. The walkway seemed to rise before him like a drawbridge. He leaned to one side, steadying himself against the trunk of a palm tree. Once again he was shaky and light-headed. He thought he might black out, so he lowered his head toward his toes. Hairy and misshapen, they were nothing at all like Indra's.

She had said that he lived in fear, that they both did, and he knew that she had meant it. He had a good idea of what it had meant for her to say it.

True Love Versus
the Cigar-Store Indian

FROM THE BACK, MONA LOOKED LIKE HUMPTY DUMPTY: A large egg-shaped trunk, pale and smooth, planted upon stumpy legs that were varicosed and bristly. Her broad head was squarish, her dark hair shorn like a boy's, feathering out just below her ears. Her neck was thick and flaccid like the rest of her body, but her arms were curiously slender and often hung stiff and lifeless at her sides. Mona was never concerned with her health, preferring fatty, tasty foods to anything even remotely wholesome. Her arms were all that kept her from being the giantess of my wildest fantasies.

"Mill," she said, examining a stack of books on my windowsill. "Utilitarianism, huh?" Her laugh was a playful squeal that seemed to come from some little girl within. She fanned herself with the book she had chosen from the middle of the stack, then settled into my rocking chair, over which hung the purple curtainlike dress she had been wearing. She flipped through the pages, pausing here and there to examine a passage. Rocking, her naked breasts sitting atop the white mass of her stomach, she reached back and pulled the dress around her shoulders like a shawl. "Was Mill for or against a free-market economy?" she asked.

Mona taught political science at Stanford, and she loved to show off, or to try to make me feel inferior, even after our affair had reached the six-month mark. It was confusing to me that she did this; in general, she didn't seem the type who needed reassurance of her intelligence and erudition. Maybe it was that she knew I was turned on by this routine of hers, by these reminders that not only was she a big woman, she was also much older than I was, my mother's age, and knew a lot more than I did, and could teach me things.

"For," I said, focusing on her plum-sized nipples.

"You're half-right. It's not really that simple. Mill argued that a free-market economy has its benefits, but he also thought that the problems that come from private ownership of production could mean that public ownership is the best answer."

I smiled inside. "I guess you're right."

"I know I am," she said, her heavy cheeks, like a bulldog's, drooping even as she grinned. She rested the book in her lap and folded her hands together, her fingers settling on scattered liver spots. I concentrated on the thick rolls of her waistline, then focused on her feet, noticing the way her toes, bloated earthworms, straddled the chair's rockers. I looked Mona in the eye, beaming, and she knew what I wanted.

"Twice in one day? My God, Nick, I'm fifty-five years old."

I was twenty-eight, and cheating on my girlfriend again, but I needed Mona. Before we met I had been spending most of my paychecks trying to pick up drunk fat women at the Tunnel Top, a sleazy bar on Bush and Stockton, around the corner from my apartment. I had spent night after night at Les Nuits de Paris, a massage parlor on the edge of the Tenderloin, where I would request "Lilly," a two-hundred-fifty-pound French behemoth who would allow me to fondle her for an extra twenty dollars. I might even follow a woman for blocks just to get a close-up look at a couple of softball-sized ankles bursting from a pair of heels. But Mona satisfied my desire, introducing me to magnificent new worlds of sexual gratification.

Allowing her dress to slip from her shoulders, she got up from the rocking chair and crawled in bed beside me. She nuzzled her head into my armpit and draped an arm across my chest. A shock of graying hair tickled my nose, smelling of shampoo and mango-scented hair spray. I cupped a love handle and felt my erection dilate beneath the dimpled fat of her inner thigh. I had never told Mona I loved her (she knew I didn't). Instead, I told her how irresistible she was. Massaging the loose flesh of her lower back, where it spilled over her tailbone to join her massive buttocks, I whispered that I wanted her.

"Let's see what we can do about that, Zeno."

Zeno—as in the famous stoic of Citium—was a nickname I had earned one evening when, after watching some PBS documentary on the psychology of grief and mourning, I said that it wouldn't much bother me if one of my close friends died, or even my mother. I told Mona about how my father had died when I was twenty-one. I was a rock now, I said, an island. When it came right down to it, I needed no one. A lie, of course, but I was never honest with Mona. I liked our relationship the way it was: simple, sexual, built upon an unspoken understanding that the real stuff of our lives need not be discussed. If I wanted a heart-to-heart I could turn to Annie, though I rarely did. I felt intensely connected to Annie due to the several years we had been together but I was often uncomfortable sharing with her anything profoundly emotional. My conscience grew guiltier every day for the way I treated her—for being repeatedly unfaithful, for stringing her along. We were together because I hadn't the fortitude to break up with her and because, in a way, I thought I was protecting her. Annie was dependent, at times clingy, unaccountably vulnerable. She needed me, or seemed to, even though she could have any man she wanted. Leaving her would be risky. Who knew how she might react? Pretending to love Annie was easier—safer—than saying good-bye. But I knew that what I was doing made me a monster, a weakling. Most of all, it made me a liar.

"Does that feel good?" Mona asked, caressing my thigh. The sensation made me shiver.

"Yes," I said. "That feels good."

"And this?" She fingered my navel, blew softly on the side of my neck.

"Yes," I said again.

"And this?" Leaning over, Mona put her tongue to my nipple and diddled it as if it were a bing cherry. She sat up and placed my hands on her breasts, and I thought, *Good God, the enormity of them.* For any other man this might have been a harrowing experience, but for me it was nothing short of rapture.

I sunk my fingers into her breasts and tried to avoid looking at her arms. Was it possible they could be so thin amid all that fat? I didn't care. I got to my knees and was about to mount Mona, when she turned and rolled from the bed.

"Where are you going?"

She waltzed across the room, her arms positioned as though she were being led, humming Vivaldi's "Al Santo Sepolcro," a sonata we both liked. She was at my window again, dragging an index finger up the stack of books. She passed and then returned to a large white volume, a collection of Montaigne's essays. Stepping back, she wound up and karate-chopped it from the stack with a piercing "Hi-yah!" knocking it and the rest of the books to the floor. "Montaigne!" she proclaimed.

"I'm taking this as a personal affront," I said.

"Don't do that, Zeno Bambino. I'm just trying to educate you. A little education before nooky never killed anyone." She could have been a stout Marilyn Monroe the way she smiled at me over her shoulder. She picked up the book and opened it. "'How the soul discharges its passions on false objects when the true are wanting.' 'By diverse means we arrive at the same end.' 'That to philosophize is to learn to die.' 'We taste nothing pure.' 'Of virtue.' 'Of sadness.' 'Of fear.' 'Of liars.' Which one?"

"'Of repentance,'" I answered. "Ask me anything about that one. I had to explicate it in front of a class my senior year in college."

"Were you naked, as you are now?"

"Clothed. I made it a habit to attend class clothed."

Mona cleared her throat. "Sit up, please. Nick Danze, sit up."

"Why don't you come back to bed now. I don't feel like discussing essays."

"Why don't you stop mouthing off and sit up straight so I can begin."

I rolled my eyes and played along, keeping in mind the ecstasy that awaited me. I was sitting up against the headboard, my erection exposed so she wouldn't forget what we were there for. Mona lifted the book like a priest exalting the Eucharist.

"'Others form man; I tell of him, and portray a particular one, very ill-formed, whom I should really make very different—'"

"'From what he is if I had to fashion him over again. But now it is done.'"

"Excuse me, young man, but we don't interrupt when someone is reading."

Mona's voice was stern and powerful, and her shoulders rose and her great breasts swelled.

"Yes, ma'am," I said. "I'm sorry, ma'am."

"Now then. Where was I? Oh, yes. 'Now the lines of my painting do not go astray, though they change and vary. The world is but a perennial movement. All things in it are in constant motion—the earth, the rocks of the Caucasus, the pyramids of Egypt—both with the common motion and with their own. Stability itself is nothing but a more languid motion.'" Mona's puckered lips spread into a smile as she stared at me over the book. She appeared proud of herself as she closed the book on her finger and walked to the bed. She was lovely. She said, "Are you in motion? Are you stable?" Her voice had lost its sternness and its power. Her tone was gentle, like a mother's.

"I'm stable," I said.

"Are you stable?" she whispered, resting the flat of her hand on my bare foot.

"I'm stable."

"Are you?"

She kissed me tenderly, running a finger up my calf. When I moved to embrace her she knocked my arm away with the heavy book.

"Since when do you make a pass at an instructor?" She looked appalled as she slid her hand up my thigh, pinched a clump of pubic hair, and wound it into a curlicue.

"OK!" I yelled. "I'm sorry!"

"That's more like it. Now sit up."

"I *am* sitting up."

"Sit up higher! Up! Up!"

I propped myself higher against the headboard. Mona released my pubic hair and reopened the book, humming Vivaldi again.

"Oh, look at this," she said. "He quotes Horace. Good old Horace. Are you a fan?"

"Of Horace?"

"Of Gladys Knight, dear. Yes, of Horace. Who else? It's not polite to engage in reverie during class." She looked down her nose, as though through spectacles. "'Why had I not in youth the mind I have today? Or why, with old desires, have red cheeks flown away?'" With that, she slammed the book on my erection and kissed me.

"Jesus Christ!" I cried, knocking Montaigne's essays to the floor. "What the fuck are you doing?"

She hooked my neck with a bony arm and kissed me again, until finally I kissed back. Then she heaved herself onto me. Digging her nails into my shoulders, she called out, "For the love of God, Zeno, I must have you! For the love of Montaigne, Horace, and God!"

I woke an hour later to the slam of the front door. Still naked, I walked to the window, kicked aside the scattered books, and watched her get into her Toyota and drive away. I looked across the street to the Yellow Indian, an old cigar store that occupied the ground floor of a four-story apartment building. I was never sure about the store's name. The big wooden Indian that guarded the place was a sun-bleached pink, once crimson, I guessed, far from yellow. The Indian's arms were folded high on his chest and his hawk eyes were half-closed and black. He wore moccasins, frayed chaps that flared from his legs, a long headdress. He had an unaffected countenance that hung solidly above his bare chest. From his shoulder hung a bow, and from his waist a satchel containing three arrows. His face was painted blue and orange and his eyes were always fixed on me—not straight ahead, but up at my window, up at me.

I had watched the Indian many times, and I figured him to be Apache. Apaches probably never carried arrows or even painted their faces, but I thought of him as Apache anyway. He looked uncompromising, unfeeling, as though he could kill a man and think nothing of it. He looked like he could hurt people, like he had the stomach for it.

When the decrepit Asian man who owned the store closed up at night, he would unchain the Indian from the bicycle rack under the window and drag him inside. The giant Apache must have weighed a couple hundred pounds, but the old man managed it every time. After the lights were turned off and the door was locked and the yellow neon sign above the door flickered out, the Apache looked out from within, his war paint illuminated by the streetlamp outside. I knew that even at night the Apache watched me. He was just as contemptible as I was, and he reminded me of everything I detested about myself.

I would look deep into him and contemplate my licentious urges and my behavior toward Annie, at times begging him out loud to stop watching me, psychotically hoping my words would have some effect. I would tell him that I wasn't going to be like him anymore, that I was going to change for the good and he would be alone in his ignobility. I knew that the solution to my troubles was to sever ties to both Annie and Mona. The only way to atone was to confess to Annie and break up with her, just as the only way to quell my fixation, I was sure, was to end my affair with Mona and deny myself the enjoyment of overweight women. I wasn't about to allow the Apache to claim me as one of his own.

The thought of being alone was terrifying. I had forgotten what it was like to be single, to suffer with no outlet from an insatiable libido. I was working as a copy editor for *Footwear Today* magazine—the same job I'd had since I was twenty-three—while trying desperately to finish the novel I was writing, five years, now, in the making. There never seemed to be enough hours in the day. I saw Mona at least three times a week and Annie almost every night, usually after her bartending shifts. I would live a lonelier life without them. Still, I had to keep telling myself that I absolutely needed to leave them. It was the only way.

Down below I saw Annie turn the corner at Bush, heading toward my building. She was smiling and radiant in the spring sunshine. She wore a small leather backpack over her shoulder, and a pink baseball cap, turned backward, hid her light-blonde hair, which she had recently begun styling like Jacqueline Kennedy's. In a white turtleneck, a short denim skirt, and a pair of patent-leather boots that rose to her knees ("kick-me-down-and-fuck-me boots," she called them), she reminded me of a Gibson girl as she moved up the block. Annie was a beauty—tall and shapely, a California girl through and through—though I had never been attracted to her the way I was to Mona. Mona could reveal the slightest fragment of skin and I was sold. With Annie I had to concentrate on how much I loved her as a

Half an hour later she had reached behind her, doing ninety at least, and brought around an orange felt hat that was shaped like a mansard roof. Annie loved hats. She had tons of them. She said that when she had a migraine they kept her head from blowing apart. Sometimes she wore an army-green homburg, sometimes a maroon tam-o'-shanter with a plastic hollyhock flower attached to the side. Presently, she removed the mansard number and tossed it in my lap. She glanced in the rearview mirror, then lifted her head just above the roll bar so the wind rearranged her hair like Einstein's. "Yeah," she said. "That air feels good. Nice and cool."

Don McLean sang "American Pie" on the radio. The horizon was streaked with oranges and reds, and I was watching the colors melt away too intently to notice that Annie was now standing on the seat, holding on to the roll bar and steering with her knees. I looked over as she closed her eyes and lifted her arms to the sky.

She was opening and closing her fingers, grabbing at the rushing air as we sailed a linear stretch of highway. To my right was a wooden guardrail, speeding by at a million miles an hour. I was too scared to say anything. Along the shoulder of the highway I saw what seemed like hundreds of black skid marks, each ending at the rail—some short, others unthinkably long, the marks of epic skids I knew must have ended in disaster.

When I looked back over I saw the Apache standing in Annie's place, his satchel of arrows inflated and flopping about in the wind. "Shit!" I screamed, stiff-arming the dash.

"Calm down, Nick," Annie said. She was steering with her hands now, lowering herself back into her seat. "I know what I'm doing. I'm not gonna kill us."

"Christ, Annie. What the hell?"

"It was unbelievable," she said. "It felt good to do that."

"Well, it scared the fuck out of me. What if you would've lost control?"

"It was just empty highway."

Annie fumbled beneath her seat until she produced the pink baseball cap, which she pulled down over her eyes. I was breathing hard. I glanced over three or four times to make sure it was still her.

We were both silent for a while. Annie seemed lost in thought. Then she said, "I'm getting tired of this, Nick."

"Of what?" I asked, knowing.

"Of this. Of our . . . situation."

"What do you need to say, Annie?"

"I don't know. I'm just not sure what I want right now."

She adjusted herself in her seat, one arm outstretched over the steering wheel. The dusk air smelled like a new tennis ball. A thin fog now veiled the highway, and the automobiles zooming by in the opposite direction sounded like crashing waves. I turned off the radio.

"What do you want?" I asked. "Think about it."

Annie turned to me, then back to the highway. "Your heart's not in it, Nick. You're not all with me. You're someplace else, always."

"Where's this coming from?" I said.

"Do you love me?" she asked.

"Of course I do. You know that."

"Is it true love? Is it real?"

I tried to imagine what true love might be like. I thought of Romeo and Juliet, Abelard and Heloise, Tom Hanks and Meg Ryan. The words *loyalty*, *maturity*, and *happiness* came to mind. I tried to picture myself making love to my soul mate, whoever she might be, but I kept thinking of Mona playing teacher that morning in my apartment, and then of her other bizarre exigencies concerning sex, not the least of which was that she claimed she couldn't come unless she secured clothespins to her nipples midway through intercourse. I saw myself beneath her as she moaned and gyrated, gearing up to grab the two clothespins from my nightstand like a pair of jumper cables.

"Yes," I lied. "It is. You feel the same, don't you?"

Annie wiped a tear from her eye. She leaned forward, pressing her chin to the steering wheel. "What is that up there?" she said.

"What?"

"In the road. Up there."

About fifteen car-lengths up was an object in the middle of the highway, an animal of some sort. Annie slowed the Jeep and pulled over as we approached it. We got out and waited while a pickup carefully circumvented what appeared to be a very large raccoon, the man and the woman inside staring the way people stare at an accident. It twitched and seemed to be trying to raise itself, but it was stuck to the highway, sealed there, it seemed, by its own leaking fluids. I could see that its head was badly mashed, grotesquely shaped like the conning tower of a submarine. The dark hair on its back, blood-spattered, was lustrous. It looked to me like one of its legs, or maybe its tail, was detached from its body.

I followed Annie to the middle of the lane. Bent over it, she said, "It's still alive, Nick."

The thing was mangled, its tail indeed severed. A vermilion goo thicker than blood seeped from its ears, and the raccoon smelled of burned rubber.

"Shit, Annie. I think this thing's had it," I said. "I'd say we should take it in, but look at it."

"You're right. Jesus."

"Let's drag it to the side of the road. Help me."

"I'm not touching that thing." Annie backed away, pinching her nostrils. "It probably has ten different diseases."

"We can't just leave it here. We've got to do something with it."

Annie looked up and down the highway, chewing her lip. "Get back in the Jeep. I'm gonna run it over. We've got to put it out of its misery."

I thought she was joking, but then I saw her head for the Jeep.

"Are you crazy?" I yelled after her. "We can't kill the thing. Just give me a hand. We'll pull it away and let it die on its own."

"I'm not pulling that raccoon anywhere, and I am not about to just leave it here to die a slow death. My head's pounding, so can we get in the Jeep and do this?"

I watched as Annie got behind the wheel and revved the Jeep. The sky was dark and a cold wind blew, swirling up from the ocean and racing across the highway. Some cars had slowed, like the pickup had, as they passed, but now the highway was calm and I heard only the legato stir of the ocean, familiar and gentle. Running over the raccoon seemed wrong, though I knew Annie had a point. Allowing it to suffer was probably just as bad.

I climbed in the Jeep. Annie gripped the steering wheel with white knuckles and stared out at the raccoon, which was no longer moving.

"I think it's dead, Nick," she said. "I think we can go."

"Are you OK?" I asked. I leaned over and felt her temples; they were hot and tender, throbbing. "Why don't I drive. You're not in any condition. You're burning up."

We switched places, and Annie removed her cap to massage the back of her head. There was now a line of about six or seven cars that were waiting to drive around the dead raccoon. I pondered what the drivers were thinking as they passed. Did they consider it something that had once been full of life? Were they saddened that it had been run over? Or was it nothing more than roadkill to them, a piece of meat impeding their journey? It did appear to be dead, but even if the raccoon was still alive, driving away seemed the right thing to do. Better, I thought, to allow it more time in this world, even if it was in critical condition, than to kill it before it was meant to die. It dawned on me that it was the simple act of living that really mattered. How much pain the thing had to endure was somehow inconsequential. It was life that was at issue here, and to take that away from it seemed unforgivable.

I leaned out of the Jeep for one last look. The raccoon was nothing but a dark mound on the highway, one end of it no different than the other.

"C'mon, Nick," Annie said. "My head's on fire."

Driving home, my mind wandering as Annie slept, I decided to start devoting real time to my novel. I was halfway into the seventh chapter, but my effort had grown desultory. I felt purposeful during the drive back to the city that night, if confused by the realization that I wasn't going to leave Annie, and that, even though she knew how I felt about her—this was clear to me now—she wasn't going to leave me either. The urge to create burgeoned within me like it never had before. I would approach my craft like a long-distance runner training for a marathon. I would write every day until the book was complete. It occurred to me that this fresh enthusiasm might be a subconscious avoidance of my futile relationship—a means of distracting myself—but it seemed truer than that. It seemed real.

I dropped Annie off, parked her Jeep, and walked the fifteen minutes back to my apartment. As I approached Powell, a cable car crawled by brimming with frenzied passengers, screams and laughter and the car's bell filling the evening air. When it passed, I watched Mona's Toyota pull away from the curb in front of my building and disappear down the hill. We hadn't planned on seeing each other, and I couldn't imagine why she might have stopped by. It wasn't like Mona to show up unexpectedly, especially on a Saturday night. Perhaps she had come to tell me that she wanted no more of our affair, in which case I would have been more than willing to agree we go our separate ways. In any event, I wouldn't contact her, and if she called I would inform her that we were through. She would understand, or pretend to. She wasn't one to carry on.

When I reached my building, the Apache was chained to the

bicycle rack under the window, vigilant as ever. The store had been closed for some time—it was well past eight o'clock—and though it seemed unlikely, the old man evidently had forgotten to bring the wooden Indian inside. I was caught off-guard by the peculiarity of the situation. The Apache was outside when he should have been in, and he appeared unusually exposed and out of place. He had the look of a left-behind child, even though his presence was as considerable as ever. He was at once fragile and menacing. I looked for some sign of recognition, but I could tell he hadn't noticed me. He was straining to find me in the shadows of my darkened apartment, searching for me where I couldn't be found. He was a creature of habit, I understood then. He was just like everyone else.

I clutched my keys, afraid to jangle them, lest he hear me. All about, in great measure, I heard the noise of life: of people and automobiles and cable cars, all part of the same life Annie lived and Mona lived and the raccoon on the highway had lived. And in the center of it all was the Apache, while I was only an arrow's shot away, paralyzed, holding my breath—there but not there.

At some point I would move. I would go upstairs and carry out my practice of drawing back the curtains and looking down upon the wooden Indian four stories below. For the time being, though, I couldn't move at all.

Glitter Gulch

Meadow dances the graveyard shift, from midnight to four. She's older than the other women, and her legs rise shapeless to broad hips and lean, veiny arms. She circles her pole, writhing in the blue-gray strobe. Nick sits at the edge of the stage sipping a Jack-and-Coke. On the floor beneath him, snug between his feet, is the shoe box from his mother's closet. Every so often he reaches down and pulls out another handful of the five-dollar casino chips, keeping his eyes on Meadow, watching as she puckers her lips or flutters her tongue between her teeth. Each time she crouches before him, leaning in to press her forehead to his, dark threads of her backswept hair fall across the bridge of his nose, and he tucks one of the chips under the lace piping of her G-string. Only up close can he tell she's pregnant.

The DJ spins a techno beat and a croaky baseline vibrates through the floor. From above, a generator releases a cloud of synthetic fog. Meadow traces her finger through her cleavage, over a dusting of iridescent powder. Her G-string is black, in contrast to her white platform stilettos. She has a small, roundish face, and Nick loves everything about it: the cleft chin, the thin lips, the retroussé nose. He loves, too, that she wears no cosmetics, makes no effort to adorn her features. Her eyes, soft and careworn, are the color of sagebrush, the fawny kind that grows behind his mother's house, on the edge of the Mojave Desert. Again Meadow crouches before him, a loose braid of hair resting on her shoulder like a tail. Nick holds up a chip, and she snatches it playfully, tossing it in a pile with the others.

"Thank you kindly," she says, tipping an imaginary hat.

Nick feels his face redden. He says nothing, only stares as she drags a finger along the inside of her thigh.

"Watching you watch me," she whispers. "It turns me on."

When Meadow's shifts have ended, after she's changed into blue jeans and a T-shirt, she unwinds with a candy bar and a can of soda in a far corner of the club. Nick often joins her at her table, hurrying over before another man approaches her. They make conversation as the other women cycle on and off the stage. She's forty-one years old, twelve years his senior. At first she was evasive about such things, but she grows more candid each time they talk. She's in the beginning of her second trimester, she's told him—week thirteen. She worries that, because of her pregnancy, she'll eventually lose her job, and complains routinely about the symptoms that have complicated her life: her cravings for junk food, her heightened sense of smell, her increased libido, her swelling breasts.

The contour of her belly is just barely distinct. Her breasts have only begun to swell. On her knees now, she shakes them back and forth. It's a contrived gesture, a service rendered, but there's an unconcealed sincerity, Nick thinks, to the way she leans into him, the way her eyelids blink enticingly to a close, the way she breathes gently against his lips.

"Whatcha got there?" she asks, her eyes squinting open, as though she's woken from a dream. She peers between his legs, pointing at the shoe box.

"Something I brought for you," he says. "A surprise."

"For me?"

"If you're good." Nick laughs uncomfortably. He isn't accustomed to teasing her this way, to being anything but biddable in her presence.

"And if I'm bad?" Meadow plays along, sucking her thumb with an affected pout. "If I'm . . . *naughty*?"

"I'll probably go ahead and give it to you anyway," he says.

The Glitter Gulch is one of the oldest striptease clubs in Las Vegas. Nick has been coming here three or four nights a week for the past two months. Concerned for his mother's well-being, he's taken a leave of absence from work and returned to his hometown. Her various addictions have cost her, in the seven years since his father's death, her financial security, her good health. While one or two flourish, the others lie dormant, diseases in remission. She's in a gambling phase right now, her compulsive shopping having given way, for the time being, to a more pernicious manner of squandering her money. Nick has come to help her in whatever way he can, hoping that his presence alone is something. He assumed, when he left San Francisco in May with an open-ended plane ticket, that he would stay only two or three weeks. But he's been sleeping in his old bedroom for two and a half months now, and though his employment is protected by the Family and Medical Leave Act, he would just as soon fly back as endure another restless night on the sunken twin-size mattress, another moment of nostalgia for his youth, another disagreement with his mother. Because they quarrel endlessly over her gambling, Nick looks forward to his late-night departures, when he slips quietly out the back door and drives his father's LeSabre twenty minutes across the city to watch Meadow dance. He looks forward, with a captive's yearning for freedom, to the time away from his mother's house.

In the shoe box is a little more than seven thousand dollars, what he assumes is his mother's latest winnings. He found the money earlier today, searching her bedroom closet for a spare hanger. The forest-green box sat on the floor among a mess of belts and shoes and laundry, its lid askew, reading *Nine West* in large beige letters. The cash was sorted into stacks of tens, twenties, fifties, and hundreds, and scattered around the stacks were five-dollar casino chips from the Golden Nugget, primrose yellow, each one emblazoned with an abstract image of Tony Bennett. He counted it out, the cash and the chips, and on an impulse he took it all, angry with his mother for having broken her latest promise to quit. It unnerves him to be responsible for so much money, and although it isn't his, he intends to give it all to Meadow.

"I solemnly swear to be a good girl," she says, raising her right hand. "Now c'mon, what do you have in there? A hamster? A new pair of heels?"

"Not a hamster," Nick says. "Not heels. We'll talk later, when you get off."

Meadow stands. "Later it is," she says, mouthing a kiss and sauntering to her pole.

There are striptease clubs, Nick guesses, where the income is enough to justify the indignity of the work, but the Glitter Gulch isn't one of them. It's dark and grungy and smells strongly of cheap perfume. Leather booths line the walls, their backrests mended with duct tape. The crowd is light for a Friday. Beneath a mirrored ceiling, Nick sits alone at the stage, a narrow peninsula that necks out into a sea of empty tables. Most of the women appear to be in their thirties. Some have acne, others wear glasses. In fifteen-minute intervals, they take turns performing on the stage and drifting around the club offering lap dances to the small audience of men. Their words are rehearsed and they display themselves with hollow smiles. There are blondes and redheads, blacks and Hispanics and Asians. But it's Meadow who Nick comes for, and he can't keep from smiling himself, fervently, without regard for composure, whenever she's near.

He remembers the first time he saw her. It was his second week back in town, and some friends from high school were meeting for drinks at a new whiskey bar in the 4 Queens. Around one o'clock, he slipped away without saying good-bye, distracted by thoughts of his mother's gambling. Walking to where he had parked his father's car, he came upon the Glitter Gulch. He knew of it, the seamy old strip-tease club at the west end of Fremont Street, but he had never been inside. It seemed the perfect diversion. It was Meadow's older age that drew Nick's attention that night, and he watched her for hours, recalling the period of his life when he was turned on by the sight of a middle-aged woman.

But when she first told him about the pregnancy—during his ninth or tenth visit, after they had talked on several occasions at her table in the corner—he felt something open inside him. She spoke softly into his ear in the middle of a lap dance. "I'm having a baby," she said, placing his hands on her buttocks, adding that she wasn't sure who the father was. She sat still at the edge of his knees. Wiping a tear from her lips, she asked him what a woman her age was doing carrying a child, her first, and suddenly, blended with a seductive sympathy, it was the notion of what she might soon look like— Meadow's physical shape as a pregnant woman—that aroused him. He didn't know why, but when he imagined her in her ninth month, belly round as a globe, an uncontainable excitement came over him. Somehow the picture in his head was enough to make her even more attractive than he already found her, in a way that seemed bizarre and prohibited. He was painfully envious of the man to whom Meadow had given herself, whoever he was. Presently, as always, Nick finds himself wishing she were farther along, showing more than she is.

She steps around her pole, caressing her belly with the flat of her hand, the strobe making it seem as though she's moving in a kind of mechanical slow motion. Then she returns to the edge of the stage, getting down on all fours and panting like a dog. Nick places one of the chips in her mouth, and she laughs, plucking it from her tongue and tossing it in the pile.

"I'm not so sure I like surprises," she tells him.

"I'm pretty confident you'll like this one."

"Give me a hint," Meadow says.

She's on her side now, propped on an elbow, running a thumb around her navel. Nick glances around the club. None of the other men seem to care that she's no longer dancing. Like him, they watch her, drinks poised in their hands, no matter what she does.

"I'm giving you," he says, "what everybody wants: peace of mind. That's all I'm going to say."

She smiles wistfully, as if discouraged by his cryptic hint. There's something about this characteristic smile of hers that makes her seem more real than the other women—more like a woman he might meet at a library or a supermarket, less like one dancing topless on a stage. The fact of her pregnancy only adds to his impression of her as an ordinary person. Still, he likes being privy to both her sides: Meadow the performer, on the job, playing a part, and—later—after-hours Meadow, sensitive and attentive, delightful. Nick has grown to rely on her companionship, and he prefers to think of her not as a hustler out to get his money but as someone who might, given the proper circumstances, take a genuine romantic interest in him. He doesn't like remembering that it's her job to make him think this way, although it's inconceivable that she might toy with his emotions. He began confiding in her early on, telling her all about the difficulty with his mother. Meadow, in turn, has entrusted him with her most intimate secret. It bothers Nick a little that she won't give him her real name: "House rule," she says each time he asks why.

But he's learned so many other things about her. That she's half Paiute Indian, half Choctaw. That, like Nick, she grew up here in Las Vegas. That she's never lived anywhere else, save for the three months she spent, in her late thirties, on a Shoshone reservation in Owyhee,

Nevada, married to a fireworks salesman she met at the Las Vegas Indian Days Festival—an adulterer and a Benzedrine addict who used to slap her around and call her a whore. Meadow hasn't dated anyone since, and a huddled agitation unfolds in Nick's chest whenever he thinks of her baby's conception as a one-night stand. It was an accident, she told him, an act of irresponsibility. She won't be receiving any child support, and talks of having no insurance, of unpaid bills for prenatal doctor visits. If only she had a little extra income, she often says, to keep her afloat. His mother's winnings should see her through the next few months, but Nick can't help wondering what she'll do after the baby is born. He's never had such an altruistic sense of purpose before, though it concurs, he supposes, with his attraction to her. Sometimes, strangely, he even imagines himself moving home to assume the role of father, giving her little boy or little girl a better life than Meadow might be able to provide on her own.

She sits up, crossing her legs, still smiling.

"You're beautiful," he tells her, as he has every other night. She rolls her eyes, and Nick finds himself devoured by an urge to make love to her during the latter stages of her pregnancy. He imagines how it might happen, a recurring fantasy—Meadow on top of him, her belly heavy against his own. He would take the belly in his hands, and she would guide his fingers along the slope of her uterus, drawing a last, slow breath before placing her lips to his, the three of them moving in balance: Nick and Meadow and Meadow's unborn baby.

But she has yet to take shape, and something like impatience trickles through him, diluting his urge. "You're as beautiful as they come," he says. "I mean it this time. I'm not just saying it anymore."

"You're punchy tonight," Meadow tells him. She cups her breasts, squeezing the nipples between her fingers, her look in some way containing both the detached confidence of a runway model and the innocent exuberance of a child. Then she touches her tongue to the tip of her nose, crossing her eyes and flapping her elbows like wings.

Nick smiles. He knows he should wait, but he reaches down, lifts the shoe box from the floor, and places it on the stage. "Like I said," he says, removing the lid just enough for her to see inside. "When you get off."

Meadow stares for a long moment. "Where'd you get all that?" she asks, her tone suddenly grave.

"It's yours," he says.

"How much is it?"

"A lot. I want you to have it."

"No," she says. "No way. Are you crazy? Close it now, please. Jesus—in a place like this?"

"It'll help you."

"Take it back home with you, Nick. It's not for me." She touches his face. "You're the sweetest, but it's not for me."

Nick replaces the lid, sets the box back down on the floor.

"Be smart," she tells him. "Put that money in the bank and don't bring it back here again."

"Aren't you something," he says. "Aren't you great."

It's past five when Nick arrives at his mother's house, frustrated that he was unable to give Meadow the money. After her shift ended, as they sat privately in the corner, he offered it a second time, but she told him, with a mixture of gratitude and exasperation, that she won't accept handouts. She isn't a freeloader, she said, isn't a charity case, but Nick is determined to bring her around. Some deeper part of him doesn't quite comprehend this determination, doesn't know why he's trying to give the money away to a woman he's known for two short months, when it could certainly be put to better use— donated, for instance, to a shelter, an orphanage—or when he could keep it for himself. Nevertheless, he wants Meadow to have it, for better or for worse. Each time he asks her out she turns him down, reminding him that, regardless of how much she might want to, she can't date customers—another house rule—and though Nick's foremost intention is to help her, he wonders if endowing her with his mother's winnings will guilt-trip her into secretly granting him a date. He knows it's selfish of him to think this way, but he can't change the way he feels about her.

He parks the LeSabre at the curb, stashing the shoe box in the trunk. On the eastern horizon, a thread of orange light outlines the uppermost peak of Sunrise Mountain, the sky whitening overhead. Las Vegas has changed so much in the decade since he moved away. Old casinos have been brought to the ground and replaced by resorts with nightclubs and theme parks. Strip malls and housing developments have unfolded in every direction, closing in on the surrounding mountain ranges that once seemed far from the city. But the neighborhood looks much the way it did when Nick grew up here: the same near-identical ranch houses, the same long-limbed saguaros and lofty, fat-trunked palm trees growing in the yards. The desert air is warm and arid, blowing past him. He watches a horned toad dart across the driveway and into the garage, the door of which has been left open. Inside, his mother's pink Mercedes—a shade darker than her house—is parked at an angle, its grille pressed up against his father's dusty ten-speed.

Nick doesn't recall the garage door being open when he left around midnight, and he guesses that his mother has only recently gotten home. Just as Nick sneaks out of the house to watch Meadow dance, his mother sneaks out to play the tables at the Golden Nugget, Binion's Horseshoe, the Plaza, preferring historic Fremont Street to what she refers to as the "Disneyized" casinos on the Strip. They've managed not to run into each other on Fremont Street, but he's caught her returning home after her trips downtown. She looks surprised to see him, guilty as a dog found soiling a carpet, though she always admits where she's been. Nick, of course, has walked in only minutes earlier—still dressed, smelling, in all likelihood, of the club—yet his mother never asks, never seems to care, why he was out. He's glad, at the present moment, that she got home before he did, and hopes he won't have to face her.

He keys in through the back door, a little drunk. The house is dark; his mother must already be asleep. Nick steps quietly to the kitchen. He's wide-awake and incredibly hungry, so he makes pancakes—he's craving them—and slices up a melon. When his mother comes in, around six, the counter is littered with crescent-shaped rinds and sluglike daubs of gray-brown batter. She rubs her eyes and says, "What are you doing up?"

"Sit down," Nick says. "Join me."

By now the room is amply lit, beams of sunlight angling through the window. His mother wears a pink silk robe, and her white slippers sweep across the tile floor.

"The smell woke me," she says.

She slides into a chair, massaging her temples with her thumbs, strands of her blondish hair falling across her eyebrows. Nick pours two glasses of orange juice, sets the table, and serves his mother breakfast.

"What am I going to owe you for this?"

"Come on," he says, settling into the chair across from her. "Enjoy."

She hurries through her meal, grinning between bites, her dark eyes bloodshot. Nick watches her chew, wondering how much she's lost overall, how much more than the seven or so thousand she would have to win to offset her numerous defeats. Blackjack is her game of choice—she's told him this—although if her luck is down she'll turn to roulette, Caribbean stud, *pai gow* poker, wasting the money from his father's life-insurance settlement. For the most part, his mother talks openly, unapologetically, about her addiction, as if to feed his worry. She sneaks out of the house, he guesses, only to avoid conflict, and because for all her impudent forthrightness, she knows in her heart that her behavior is indefensible.

Nick sips his orange juice, pours syrup over a second helping of pancakes. Feeling sober now, he wants to talk about the shoe box. He knows he shouldn't have taken it from his mother's closet. What's more, he's still angry with her, and feels he should tell her so, even though the thought of an argument makes him queasy.

"Did you go somewhere last night, Mom? Did you go downtown again?"

"Great pancakes," she says.

"I know it feels like I'm pestering you, but we don't seem to be getting anywhere here." He speaks softly, carefully. "You've taken no positive steps at all to—well, to help yourself."

She must have noticed the box's absence by now, he thinks, must have noticed, if she did in fact go out last night, the absence of his father's car. But she only says, "For fuck's sake, Nicky. I'm all talked out about that." She reaches for an ashtray, a book of matches, and a pack of Marlboros, lined up on the counter in front of the telephone.

"OK," Nick says feebly, "I know, but—"

"Please," she says, lighting a cigarette, and they're both silent for a while.

During previous visits, he's found comp slips, players-club cards, Ziploc bags stuffed with chips from her favorite casinos. His mother laughed, shrugging her shoulders, when she first told him about losing money from the settlement. Though occasionally she wins, sooner or later she wagers whatever wealth comes her way. Each time she's promised to quit—halfheartedly, placatingly—she's called him two or three weeks later from a pay phone, at his office or late at night at his apartment, hollering into the receiver, slot machines dinging in the background, coins clanging into pay wells. "Your mother's back in it, Nicky, and she's winning like a champ," she told him once. Another time she said, "Guess who just made two grand in an afternoon."

"You're one to talk," she says now. "How's the book coming along? I haven't seen you working on it once since you got here."

Seven years later, he's still grinding away at the novel he began after college, a long, amorphous account of his days as a student at USC. He told his mother he was taking off work to complete the remaining chapters with maximum effort: his excuse for coming home. In truth, Nick is grateful for the time away. Working all day as a copy editor often leaves him too weary of the written word to make any nighttime headway on the novel. He has gotten some writing done in the course of his stay, but until now she hasn't inquired about his progress.

"Forget about me," he says. "It's you we're focusing on."

"Listen, Nicky. I'm changing every day. I'm different lately. Let me put it like this: I understand the error of my ways." She fixes her eyes on the tile, as if reading from a teleprompter at their feet. "If there's one thing I've learned since your father's been gone, it's that nothing's going to save you from your life. Faith alone won't save you. Sometimes you need to reinvent yourself in order to survive."

"What are you saying?" he asks her. "You were just out at the casinos last night, were you not?"

"I'm saying I'm no longer the person I used to be."

"You need professional help, Mom. You need to move away from here, go someplace new."

She exhales, fanning the smoke. Her addiction to nicotine has worsened in recent years, and it rankles to watch her. She's developed a cough and a wheeze, much like the ones Nick's father had before he died.

"I took the money," Nick says, unsure of what he'll say if his mother wants it back. "I took the box in your closet."

"I saw that." She knits her forehead, as though working a crossword puzzle. "Keep it. Buy yourself something nice. Because whatever I do next with my life, it won't take money or possessions to do it. I know that much. It won't take this house, or this table here, or this robe," she says, voice raised. She tugs at the sleeve of her robe, picks up her fork and slams it down on the table. "You can trust me on that."

Nick has no idea what she's talking about. "I'm going to be staying another week or so, Mom," he says. "I can't leave you like this."

She shakes her head at the floor, and Nick envisions a future in which his life has fallen back into place, in which he's returned to his apartment, his job, even though it's onerous and dizzying to think of leaving Meadow behind. His mind skips from one thought to the next, landing on an image of his father. Nick thinks about the kind of person his mother was when he was growing up, before the fibrosis developed in his father's lungs—he remembers her belonging to a health club, playing the violin, chatting with mail carriers and sales clerks—then about the kind of person she is now, some alternate version of herself, some woman he doesn't know, doesn't wish to know. For the past seven years, season after season, he's been returning home to care for her in one way or another, but this latest visit, he realizes, has been entirely in vain. In two and a half months he's done nothing tangible to help her.

"All I know is that things won't be the same around here," she says, speaking in a whisper as she often does after she loses her temper: her "voice of reason," she likes to call it. It's a practice that isn't so much an expression of calmness, Nick thinks, as it is a stagy eccentricity. "I've come to understand that I'm not the person I thought I was. Does that make better sense, Nicky?" She looks at him sternly. "Does that make sense?"

"Did you hear what I said, Mom?"

"Stay," she says, hacking as she stubs out her cigarette. "Stay if you have to." She closes her eyes and takes a breath, and for some reason Nick thinks that she, too, is picturing his father. "I'm through," she says. "With all of it."

<-<-->->

He tells his mother he'll be in his bedroom working on the novel, but he sleeps away the rest of the morning. When he wakes, around two, he finds a Post-it stuck to the refrigerator: *Went for a drive.* Replaying their early morning conversation in his head, he wonders if she really is making an effort to change. But the hours tick by, and she doesn't return, doesn't call, and he's sure his mother has spent her entire Saturday at a casino. By midnight Nick still hasn't heard from her, though he knows she's only lost track of time, placing wager after wager.

He arrives at the Glitter Gulch just before one. On the stage, Meadow is crawling around on her hands and knees, out of sync with a fast-paced disco number. She wears black suede boots, a leopard-print G-string with a tasseled waistband. Nick takes his usual seat. He orders a Jack-and-Coke from a passing cocktail waitress, stowing the shoe box on the floor between his feet. It's unkind of him, he thinks, not to return his mother's winnings, but he knows she would only lose it all at the tables. Besides, Meadow is worse off than his mother, or soon will be. He wants the money in her possession before he leaves town.

Beside him sits a biker with tattooed arms and a long, dark beard. He's thickset and wears black leather chaps and a faded denim vest that reads *Harley-Davidson* across the back. "Not too shabby, is she?" the man says, turning to Nick with a smile, a bottle of beer gripped in one hand.

"I'm sorry?" says Nick.

"If she lost a few pounds, that is. Either way, though."

Nick nods and looks away. He feels an instinctual, protective aggravation, though he remains silent. The cocktail waitress returns with his drink. As he pays her, he can see in his peripheral vision that the man is still staring at him.

"Billy Merrin," the man says in a deep, stentorian voice. He's maybe forty—a Hells Angel, Nick surmises, or an Outlaw. A part runs like a riverbed through the center of his hair, and an orange bandana, folded into a headband, hides his eyebrows.

"Hello," Nick replies, keeping his focus on Meadow. She's on her feet now, wrapping herself around her pole, kicking her legs like a Rockette. Nick hears the man swig from the bottle, the bubbly flush of beer as he lowers it from his mouth.

"How do you think she manages to move around that good in those boots of hers?" asks the man. "So pointed she could kick a goddamn ant in the ass."

Nick ignores him, watching as Meadow struts to the edge of the stage and crouches before them. She pinches her nipples, whips her braid back and forth across her shoulders.

"How much?" the man barks, rapping on the stage with his knuckles. "How much for a little one-on-one attention?"

"Twenty bucks," Meadow says. "But you'll have to wait until I'm all done up here."

"I'm not talking about a lap dance. I'm talking about later tonight, after you're off work."

She gives him a hateful look, glances at the bouncer near the door. "Fuck off," she tells him. "I'm not for sale."

The man belches, leaning toward Nick, smelling of patchouli and leather. Under his breath, he says, "I'll kill that bitch, talking to me like that." A moment later he laughs, kicking at the stage. "I'm tanked," he says. "Don't believe a word I say." He finishes his beer, waves a hand at Meadow. Then he stands, stretching his arms, and Nick watches him stagger through the tables and exit the club.

"Easy there," Meadow says, as though she's read Nick's mind. "I know how to handle myself against an asshole like that."

Later, they sit together at her corner table, the shoe box resting in Nick's lap. Meadow is wearing her blue jeans, her T-shirt. She's eating a Snickers bar and drinking from a can of Sprite, her dark hair set loose, falling like a shoulder cape around her upper arms. The music is slow, an R & B ballad with a saxophone solo, and a skinny blonde with a pageboy hairdo has taken the stage.

"I know you're proud," Nick says, "and I admire that. But I want you to have this money." He places a hand on the box. "It'll give you a fresh start, get you out of the hole you're in. What are you going to do otherwise?"

"Nick." Meadow offers him a glum smile.

"It's a gift," he says, "not a loan."

"There's something you have to know."

She runs a hand over his forearm, squeezes his wrist. All night she's seemed reserved, and Nick has had a nagging hunch that she's keeping something from him, that something terrible has happened— that she's miscarried, or aborted the fetus. He braces himself for what he's about to hear.

"I feel awful about it, but I haven't been honest with you," she confesses. "I'm not a good person, Nick."

Then she tells him what, deep down, he's somehow known all along, what he's sensed, really, but hasn't allowed himself to believe: that there never was a baby. She invented her pregnancy, she explains, in hopes that as he got to know her better he might take pity on her, a poor, middle-aged topless dancer about to become a single mother. In actuality, she's still married to the Shoshone, she says, an ex-convict, a scam artist, whose idea it was for her to swindle one of her customers.

"I told him about your mother's inheritance—settlement, I mean—what's left, at least. He thought we might be able to get our hands on some of it before you went back to San Francisco. It was a stupid plan, saying I was pregnant. I told him it would never work. But once it did, once you actually tried to give me all that money last night, I couldn't go through with it." She stares at the shoe box, shaking her head. "He kept saying I should go out with you, sleep with you," she says, "but I wasn't willing to stoop that low. I think of you as a friend, Nick. All I want now is for you not to hate me."

Nick doesn't speak, astonished by his own gullibility. He contemplates the extent of her deceit: the symptoms she complained about, the way she cried when she first told him she was pregnant, the slight paunch she led him to believe contained a fetus. She's right—their plan *was* stupid, a ridiculous scam, and yet he fell for it. She's a hustler after all, he thinks. He should tell her off, demand she reimburse him for all the tips he's given her over the past two months. But as his mind goes round and round, it wanders, for some reason, to his mother's unhappy recklessness, to everyone else suffering in the world, and he decides he won't make Meadow feel any worse than she already does. His sensitivity seems a weakness. Only a fool would make allowances for her behavior—a fool, that's what he is—though he can't help considering the starkness of her life. Her job here at the Glitter Gulch, her marriage to a manipulative criminal who may or may not be unfaithful, drug-addicted, and abusive. Even after her confession, her misfortune finds its way to his heart, his interest in her reinforced, baby or no baby, and he realizes that what he feels for Meadow is love—not romantic love, in spite of his attraction to her, but the sort he feels for his mother, heavy, inert, suspended inside him like a hanged man from a gallows. There's probably more to the situation than what Meadow has told him, but in an instant he's forgiven her.

"I tried to take advantage of your kindness," she says. "I knew how much you liked me." Again she squeezes his wrist. "My real name's Janet," she tells him. "I'm sorry, Nick. My life isn't where I want it to be right now."

Before he can respond, the door of the club swings open and the biker steps back in. He spots Nick and Meadow, and makes his way toward their table, nodding as he moves across the floor. He takes a seat between them, reeking, now, of beer, and drops his hands on his thighs. "What I want to know," he says, sneering at Meadow, "is who the fuck you think you are."

"I'll get rid of him," Meadow says, looking toward the bouncer, a large Middle Eastern man in a tight black tank top and shiny gray pants.

"No," says Nick. "Wait a minute. Let's not make a scene out of this. Is there something we can help you with?"

"*Is there something we can help you with?*" the man says, aping him. "I changed my mind," he says to Meadow, and strokes his beard. "You're not so good-looking after all."

"All right," Nick says. "Enough now." But the man, Merrin, isn't listening; he's leaning closer to Meadow, telling her she ought to treat people with the respect they deserve. Beneath the table, Nick clenches his fists. All of a sudden he's ready to throw a punch, not just for Meadow's sake but also because he can't shake the thought that he's a fool. He remembers his father calling him a sucker for having lost fifty dollars in a pyramid scheme his senior year of high school, and feels a familiar itch to commit an act of violence, the way some people feel in electronics stores, fantasizing, for no good reason, about smashing the screens of televisions with a baseball bat. He's felt it, this itch, here at the Glitter Gulch, and at his mother's house, and driving to and from Fremont Street when he's wanted nothing more than to steer the LeSabre over the median and crash it into an oncoming automobile. Now he wishes to beat Billy Merrin with every atom of his body. He stands, tucking the shoe box under his arm. As loud as he can, unable to withhold his anger, he says, "I told you that's enough."

Merrin stands too. "What if we talk about this outside," he says, spitting the words.

"After you," says Nick, surprising himself. It electrifies him, this undaunted response of his, though his voice is shaky, his stomach knotted tight.

"Hey," Meadow says. "C'mon, Nick. He's drunk." Again she looks toward the bouncer.

"Don't," Nick tells her. "I can handle this."

She calls after him as he follows Merrin across the club, but Nick doesn't turn, his feet brick-heavy by the time he's reached the door, his arms tingling as though from goose bumps.

Outside, Merrin narrows his eyes and says, "What's in the box?"

Nick looks silently at him, setting the shoe box on the sidewalk. It's after four, but Fremont Street, off-limits to automobiles, is busy with pedestrians, vendors of all kinds, Hispanic men handing out flyers for peep shows and escort agencies. The air smells of roasted peanuts. Nick can hear Merrin breathing, a faint, gurgle-like snore.

"You want to dick around with me? I asked you a question." As if calling a dog, Merrin smacks the side of his thigh, skin jiggling above his elbow. "What's in the goddamn box?"

Nick still doesn't answer him, his anger erased by an unexpected impotence. Despite his itch for violence, he's not a fighter, not a confrontational person. He hasn't a clue what to do or say. Fear takes hold of him as he remembers schoolyard skirmishes from his childhood, classmates crowded around him, clapping and hollering as his heart beat wildly and he tried to recall the proper way to make a fist.

Now Merrin is in his face, squeezing his arm, twisting it—impossibly, it seems. Somebody yells for them to take it easy, but pain explodes in Nick's ear. It's happened so fast: he's been punched two, maybe three times. Light streams through his field of vision, the noise of the street muffled as though he's under water. Merrin steps toward the shoe box—a blur of motion—as Nick lunges for his neck, his chest, the tattooed flesh of his shoulder. Again Merrin punches him, this time in the temple. Nick feels his legs buckle, feels himself falling.

When he comes to, Meadow and the bouncer are squatted next to him. There's a drumming in Nick's forehead, a fiery twinging around his ear. Several people have stopped to watch him. The lights of the casinos, like a million cameras, flash all around.

The bouncer takes his hands, helps him to his feet. "Slowly," he says, looking into Nick's eyes. "Can you see me all right?"

"I think so. Yeah."

"For God's sake," Meadow says. "We have to call an ambulance."

A lump has formed at Nick's temple. He pokes it with his thumb, presses its tender edges. "No ambulance," he says, the lump throbbing vigorously now. "I'll be fine."

"Why don't you come inside and have a seat," says the bouncer.

Nick looks around for the shoe box. "Where'd he go?"

"Took off, I guess," the bouncer says, shrugging, looking at Meadow. "I really think you should come in and sit down."

But Nick pushes past them, past the onlookers, and weaves his way through the crowd, making a frantic search for the box. Billy Merrin is nowhere in sight, and after a time Nick circles back to the Glitter Gulch, tapping the angry lump.

Only Meadow is waiting. She's gotten him a plastic freezer bag filled with ice cubes. "He stole the money, didn't he?"

She gives him the bag, and he presses it to his head. "It's gone," he says.

Meadow covers her mouth with her hand. "We need to call the police."

"Was that him? Was that your husband?"

"My *husband*? No, Nick. I swear it wasn't."

"Whatever. Let's just forget about it."

"We can at least—"

"Seriously," he says, and again it overcomes him, the infuriating knowledge of his own foolishness. "The money's gone."

"I'm so sorry this had to happen," she tells him. "All of this, everything."

He can hear in her voice genuine remorse, and he's filled, now, with shame, as if her emotions have somehow fused with his own.

"This whole situation," she says. "It's all my fault."

Nick hears himself say, "It is what it is," an expression he hates.

"Thanks for sticking up for me." Meadow leans in awkwardly and kisses his cheek. "You sure you're OK?" she asks.

He raises his hand in a wave, sickened: he knows he'll never see her again. He misses her already, wants to hug her, hold her in his arms. Instead, he says, "I need you to go."

"It wasn't all lies," Meadow says. "I've never told anyone some of the things I told you."

But Nick repeats it, as kindly as he can: "I need you to go." There's nothing more he can bring himself to say, and Meadow turns quickly and walks back inside the club.

He leans against a palm tree that grows from a circular plot in the sidewalk, and at this instant, lowering the bag from his head, he sees his mother, not twenty yards away, striding purposefully through the crowd, heading toward the entrance of the Plaza.

She's wearing khakis and what Nick recognizes as one of his father's shirts, ill-fitting and untucked, a short-sleeved oxford with pinstripes. As he watches her hasten up the other side of the street, Nick feels the way he might feel upon sighting a celebrity: adrenalized, dumbstruck. He doesn't want her to see him here, yet he feels a curious need to call her name. He can't ignore it. "Liz!" he yells, ducking behind the palm tree. "Elizabeth Danze!"

He sneaks a look. She appears not to have heard him, entering the brightly lit casino through the sliding glass doors, purse held to her side. But when he calls her again, yelling "Mom" this time, she wheels around and walks back out. He decides to show himself—he feels he has to—and so he steps out from behind the tree. He catches only glimpses of her now: people are passing on the sidewalk in front of her, and she's on tiptoe, peering over them, looking everywhere but where he's standing.

She walks back toward the entrance of the casino, the glass doors sliding open. A second later she's gone.

This Life or the Next

THEY FOUND HIS MOTHER ASLEEP ON THE COUCH, A BOX OF sugar propped between her knees. One end of its top had been lifted open, peeled back like a length of bark, and the lap of her pink silk robe held a dusting of spilled crystals that caught the light of an end-table lamp. She was slouched and snoring, head tilted to the side. In a corner of the room the local news murmured from the television. At her slippered feet stood a second open box.

Nick looked at Annie, who studied his mother with a raised eyebrow. It was Valentine's Day, and they had just returned from a late dinner downtown.

"Mom," he said, placing a hand on his mother's shoulder, shaking it gently. On the cushion next to her was a heart-shaped greeting card. It lay closed, facedown, but he knew it was from his father. She still had every card Nick's father had ever given her stacked neatly in her nightstand drawer.

"Mom," Nick repeated, and her eyes fluttered open. She gave a start, drawing her legs together, kicking over the box at her feet.

Nick bent down and picked it up. It was identical to the one between her knees: yellow and white, the brand name, Domino, printed in a cartoonish script, electric-blue letters that ballooned diagonally across the cardboard. The box was empty, and its near-weightlessness made it seem as though he were holding a stage prop, something, at any rate, meant to appear heavier than it was. To his right, Annie remained silent. They had been in Las Vegas since Friday, staying in Nick's old bedroom, but this was the first either of them had seen of the sugar. Not for lack of trying. Nick, in secret, had searched cupboards, closets, drawers. He had looked behind furniture, beneath her bed, in the trunk of her car, certain his mother had stowed it all away.

"Jesus," he said. "Look at you."

His mother stared at him, expressionless. "You're home early," she said.

"It's almost eleven." He sat down on a corner of the coffee table. Wind shook the windows, whistling against the glass. On one of the sills stood a tall ceramic vase of wilted chrysanthemums. "You'll kill yourself," he told her. "Is that what you want?"

His mother didn't answer. She smoothed her robe over her thighs, sweeping the sugar from her lap. She liked to drink it straight from the box, or eat it cube by cube. At first, in the months directly following his father's death, eating sweets had been her comfort, a means, she had said, of alleviating grief. She would sit in front of the television and indulge herself, just as she had tonight, and before long she would forget, if only temporarily, the new circumstances of her life. But the candy and pastries his mother had gluttonously consumed were no longer enough. Pure cane sugar was all she wanted. She often ate three or four pounds a day, sometimes nothing else. Her cravings, she had told him, were uncontrollable, and Nick had simply to look at her for proof. Over the past couple of years, his mother had put on more than a hundred pounds. Her face was plump, shaped vaguely like an eggplant, her back broad and pillowy. Loose skin hung from her arms, dimpled around the elbows, and at her waistline was a thick outgrowth of fat.

"Hi, Mrs. Danze," Annie ventured, fingering the long string of pearls that hung around her neck. She wore a sable shift and matching heels, and suspended from her shoulder was a red leather purse the size of a small camera bag, her hair trained into a girlish pigtail that sprouted like a pom-pom from the back of her head. They had met before, when his mother had visited him in San Francisco, but this was Annie's first trip to Las Vegas.

"Nick likes to remind me that I have a problem," his mother said with a smile, the other box still between her knees. "I'm sure he's filled you in."

"I thought we'd made a little progress," Nick said. He searched his mother's face for some sign of contrition, but found nothing. "Not so, I guess." Where, he wondered, had she hidden the two boxes?

"I'll leave you both alone," said Annie.

"No," he told her. "You're fine, hon."

They had eaten dinner at a new restaurant she had seen profiled in the Travel section of the *Chronicle*—an expensive, scantily decorated place a couple of miles from the Strip—and as Nick had looked around at the other patrons, most of whom had worn pink or red or some integration of the two, he realized with a warm wave of pride that Annie was the most appealing woman in the room, with her blonde hair and blue eyes and small, lapidary features. Nick couldn't believe that he wasn't attracted to her, that in the seven years they had been together he had never fallen in love with her—that he cheated on her with such fiendish regularity. He hadn't wanted Annie to come with him to Las Vegas, but she had pressed him, claiming he needed her for emotional support, and Nick had given in. In recent years he had let pass—gutlessly, he thought—numerous opportunities to end their relationship. That she was here at his side only confirmed her place in his life, and he felt a stale disenchantment float through him, his sense of himself as a coward.

"You look beautiful tonight, Annie." His mother rubbed her eyes. Her robe, as she shifted on the couch, strained to cover her bulging stomach. "Can I get you something to drink? Some tea, maybe?"

"Oh, I'm fine," Annie said. "But thank you."

"We don't want anything to drink, Mom."

"I wasn't talking to you," his mother said. She scratched the tip of her nose, brushing from her forehead a dark mass of hair. It fell from her head in strands of black and gray. She had neglected it over the past year—failing to have it dyed its usual sandy blonde, failing to have it cut, its lengthening seeming to keep pace with the steady expansion of her waistline.

Nick got up, walked around the coffee table, and sat back down. "Don't you have anything to say for yourself?" he said, plucking the box from between his mother's knees. It, too, was empty.

"I need it," his mother said. "Is this what you have to hear? It takes the edge off, Nicky. Better than those damn pills I was on."

It was true, then, that she had stopped taking her medication. Since Friday he had been waiting for the right moment to ask her about it, as she always grew snappish when he probed. Every so often he checked with his mother's pharmacy, phoning long-distance, to make sure she was picking up her prescriptions—Zoloft and Desyrel—and the last time Nick had done so, he had been told that her most recent refill remained uncollected. This was the reason he and Annie had come. He had figured February was as good a time as any to make a trip home, telling his mother that Annie wanted to get away for the holiday and had always wished to visit Las Vegas.

"You aren't supposed to be off those pills," he said now, sounding defeated, he thought. He couldn't help feeling responsible—guilty, really—for the shape his mother was in. He should have moved back home a long time ago. Although he visited often, his absence, he knew, was somehow related to her worsening condition. He hated the weary, pitiless side of himself that grew aggravated with her like this, even though his aggravation was born only of concern. For some time now he had been acting more like a warden than a son, stern and watchful, intolerant of her weakness—distance, in the main, keeping their relationship intact—and he feared what might happen were he ever to move back to Las Vegas: that in becoming his mother's keeper he would grow to resent her, and she him. He considered how liberating it would be to leave her to her own devices, however guilty he might later feel.

"What about your therapist?" Nick set the two empty boxes on the coffee table, sighing. A foul odor wafted from the chrysanthemums, their petals flagging against their stems. "I assume you're still seeing her, at least."

"You look just like him," his mother said. "Sitting like that, I mean. You've got your father's posture."

"Don't do that," Nick told her. "Don't bring him up to change the subject."

"Nick," said Annie.

"He's on my mind," his mother said.

There were framed photographs of his father everywhere he looked: on the tables and walls, the shelves, the mantle above the fireplace. His mother hadn't stopped wearing her wedding ring, a gold band that held a brilliant Asscher-cut diamond, and was convinced that his father communicated with her—"obliquely, like God"—via the flickering of streetlamps, the warbling of birds.

"You need to stop thinking about Dad and start thinking about yourself," Nick said. Immediately, he regretted saying it.

"I'm going to bed now," his mother said sharply, "if we're done here." She got up from the couch, slipping the greeting card into a pocket of her robe. "It's nice to have you with us, Annie. I'm sorry you have to be a part of this."

Nick walked to a window, peered through the open curtains. It had been cold and damp since they had arrived, mist swirling from a charcoal sky, and he watched as wind drove rain against a fan palm in the front yard. On the television, the news had ended and an infomercial had begun, a woman's voice describing the various benefits of a dietary supplement. Nick wished he had gotten his mother a gift for the holiday. She had declined his invitation to join them for dinner—handing him a key to the house, telling them to stay out as late as they wanted—and it pained him to think of her at home by herself on Valentine's Day, scarfing down sugar and staring at an old card from his father.

Without his noticing, Annie had walked up beside him. She cleared her throat, threaded her fingers through his.

"I'm trying to save your life," Nick said, turning from the window, but his mother had already left the room.

The next day, Nick and Annie drove north across the valley, sailing along the rain-slick streets in his father's LeSabre. It was a Monday afternoon, but the city seemed barely inhabited, the traffic sparse, the sidewalks empty, as though, in anticipation of some natural disaster, people had fled to the suburbs. Annie had a list of attractions she wanted to check out on the Strip: the Forum shops at Caesars Palace, the roller coaster at New York–New York, the observation deck at the Stratosphere. She had been in a buoyant mood throughout the weekend, even though they had done little more than visit with his mother, but now she seemed pensive—downcast, Nick thought. He caught her staring silently at the glove compartment, blinking her eyes as if she were about to cry. When he began to talk about his mother, she reached across the console to rest a hand on his knee.

"She's still in so much pain," Annie said, biting her lip. She wore tight blue jeans, a red cable-knit sweater, and a yellow cycling cap, its frayed bill flipped up to reveal her high, freckled forehead. "She needs a diversion, something to take her mind off her life."

"Everything seemed to be going so well with the drugs. To think I was foolish enough to believe she was getting better."

Two years had passed since Nick had first realized the magnitude of his mother's addiction, happening upon her in the kitchen with her mouth to a bowl of sugar, her head tipped back as if she were chugging from a carton of milk. He had been home on one of his routine visits and had gotten up in the middle of the night for a glass of water. It had been like seeing her naked, so startling was the moment. He still found himself bewildered by her lust for sugar—how bizarre it was! He had researched the possible side effects besides obesity: hypoglycemia, diabetes, tooth decay, heart disease, gallstones, cystic fibrosis, arthritis. The list went on. How was it that his mother was still grieving after eight long years? Nick himself had loved his father dearly, but he had dealt with the loss, or thought he had. It was easier for him, his mother said. "You can't imagine what it's like," she had once told him, "to lose a spouse," as if losing his father had been no different than the day Kepler, his cairn terrier, had died, during Nick's senior year in high school. His mother wouldn't remarry—not now, she said, not ever—and Nick wondered if she had any desire at all to change her life, to be helped. He and Annie were to return to San Francisco tomorrow afternoon. Even if his mother did want his help, what could he do for her in the next twenty-four hours? What could he say? He had come without a plan, an impetuous response to the news from her pharmacy, and now his visit—like so many others, and complicated by Annie's presence—was amounting to nothing.

As they made a left onto Flamingo Road, Annie craned her neck to look at the Spring Mountains, capped in hazy white and looming on the distant horizon, rising like a tidal wave behind the city. Rain blurred the windows of his father's car. When they reached the Strip, she said, "Vegas. Of all the places for you to be from."

"I still feel bad I didn't move back here after my dad died," Nick said, though he had never mentioned this to her before. "I've been considering it, coming home to stay. My mom needs me around. She's lonely, that's all."

He waited to see the disappointment in her face, her fear at the idea of losing him to his mother. Annie lowered her head and said, "You're not what she's looking for."

At Caesars Palace, Nick left the LeSabre with a parking attendant and they walked through a small crowd toward the entrance, a wet wind sweeping over them. Inside, he led Annie past the reception desk and into the casino, where banks of slot machines stretched toward clusters of blackjack tables, roulette tables, and craps pits. Bells sounded as coins clattered into pay wells. Beside an escalator, a group of women posed for a photograph with three brawny men costumed as Roman gladiators. Cocktail waitresses hurried around in dark Cleopatra wigs.

"I think the Forum shops are that way," Nick said, pointing.

"First I want to play," said Annie. "Just for a bit. Just a couple hands."

"'A couple hands'? When have you ever gambled?"

She took his arm. "We're in a casino, baby."

"I guess it wouldn't hurt to lose a few bucks on the way," he said hesitantly. It bothered him that, like his mother, she was so cavalier about money—unwilling to open a savings account, charging whatever she couldn't pay for. "No cards, though," he said. "The players get mad when you don't know the rules." He looked around, considering their options. "Roulette," Nick said. "That's our game."

They made their way to a table in the center of the room. As they took their places at two vacant stools, Annie whispered, "We can't ever become like that."

"Like what?"

"That," she said, pointing with her chin. Just beyond the table, an elderly couple, hunched and dead-eyed, fed coins into two slot machines. "All the excitement gone. Nothing left to say to each other. We gotta have some spirit in us when we're old and gray."

Lately, with increasing frequency, Annie had been making comments that implied a future they would inevitably share. She spoke of a spring wedding, a honeymoon in Tahiti, the two-story brick house in which they would live and the several children that would eventually occupy its bedrooms. She would smile dreamily, as if it were only a matter of time before her expectations were realized. "I'm your one true love," she would tell him. In response, Nick would tug at his earlobe or scratch his chin, looking thoughtful, he hoped, while saying nothing.

"The key," she said, "is communication. You have to want to talk to one another in order to keep a marriage alive."

Nick sniffed, nodding his head. He tried to envision growing old with Annie but could conjure no images of the two of them as a married couple. His friends in San Francisco loved her. They took turns asking him when he was going to propose, what he was waiting for. His mother, despite the limited amount of time she had spent with Annie, seemed fond of her as well, allowing her to sleep with Nick in his bed, complimenting her haircut, her outfits, her smile. From time to time Annie pressured Nick to move in with her, but he had grown adept at putting her off. He kept waiting for their relationship to come to a natural end. In fact, he had come to rely on Annie, and although he wasn't able to imagine her as his wife, he had been with her for so long that he could scarcely conceive of a life without her. She showed him nothing but devotion, and it troubled him that he continued to lead her on, and that his infidelities were so numerous. He had sworn to himself that he would never hurt her—never allow Annie to discover the truth about him. Still, he was convinced that somehow she already had. That she knew he was something of a louse when it came to being faithful, knew he didn't deserve her, knew he only loved her the way he might a cousin or a close friend.

"Here they are on vacation, I bet," she said somberly, still watching the couple, "and they're not even talking. Just pouring all their money into those machines."

"One-armed bandits," Nick said, and took out his billfold. The dealer was a tall, bearded man, and Nick handed him two twenty-dollar bills. "We lose those," he said, "and we're done."

"We'll see," said Annie.

The dealer slid the bills into the drop box and stacked eight red chips on the felt, pushing the stack across the layout. The minimum bet was five dollars. Tables with such low minimums often attracted the largest crowds, though this one was empty but for a thick, square-shouldered man in a black Stetson, who sat picking his teeth with the nail of his middle finger.

"I like your hat," Annie said to him.

"It was a gift," the man said, "from my wife." He wore a black suit and a white button-down, and from his neck hung a black bolo tie, its clasp a bronze medallion that flickered as he tipped the hat. "Buys me a different one every year for my birthday."

Annie's own collection of hats crowded the closets of her apartment, fedoras and porkpies and trilbies rising from shelf to ceiling in cockeyed stacks. Nick had only recently grown accustomed to her practice of wearing one almost everywhere she went. With little room in her suitcase, she had packed only the yellow cycling cap, leaving behind the early Valentine's Day gift he had given her, a vintage leghorn he had found at a thrift shop in Noe Valley, its red plaited straw in near-perfect condition.

"Your wife has good taste," Annie said.

The man gave a smile. "Why I married her."

Nick explained the various ways of placing a bet, talking into

Annie's ear. "Don't get your hopes up," he said. "In the end, the house always wins."

"Such the pessimist."

"You mean realist," Nick said.

They played only the number seven, Annie's idea—not because the number was considered lucky, she said, but because of the seven years they had been together as a couple.

"Six and a half," Nick corrected her.

The man in the hat played streets and corners, crowding the layout with his twenty-five-dollar chips. The wheel was made of a dark, glossy wood, its ivory numbers blurring as it spun, the silver ball bouncing from fret to fret before settling with a rattle into one of the canoes. In a short time Nick's forty dollars was gone.

"So much for seven," he said, trying to sound nonchalant. He was irritated and wanted his money back. "To the Forum we go."

Annie stared, unblinking, at the wheel.

"It's not like we lost my father's car," Nick said.

"How long have you been married?" she said, turning to the man in the hat.

"Thirty-one years this June."

"How'd you know?" Annie asked him. "How'd you know she was the one?"

"Annie. Hon." She was trying to make some kind of point, Nick thought, trying to make him feel bad that in all the time they had been together he hadn't once told her he wanted to spend the rest of his life with her, hadn't so much as hinted at the prospect of marriage.

"Leap of faith," said the man. "You don't need me to tell you that." He lifted the hat, scratched the crown of his head, a thin band of his graying hair ironed flat. At his neck, the hair bristled like quills. "I knew I loved her, of course. But still."

Annie watched as the man cleared the layout of his winnings and placed a hundred-dollar chip on red. He had doubled his money since they had sat down, and Nick suspected he felt invincible, wondering what allowed the man to dress the way he did, like Gene Autry or Roy Rogers. Nick envied his speech, loud but measured, as well as the sureness with which he placed his bets, clicking his tongue, patting the felt with the tips of his long, fleshy fingers. Lately, Nick hadn't felt sure of anything, not really, and he pondered what singular wisdom might account for the man's confidence.

"I want to keep playing," Annie said, removing her wallet from a pocket of her blue jeans.

"Come on," Nick said. "This is a sucker's game."

"Not for our friend here, it isn't."

The man laughed through his nose, shifting his eyes beneath the hat's wide, concave brim as Annie handed the dealer a wrinkled hundred-dollar bill.

"We're only going to lose more money," Nick whispered.

"'We'?" she said. "This is *my* money I'm playing with."

The dealer pushed two stacks of chips across the layout. Annie placed both the stacks, all twenty of the five-dollar chips, on the number seven.

"Whoa," said Nick. "Have you lost your mind?"

The man in the hat lifted his eyebrows and the dealer spun the wheel. Annie looked on, tight-lipped, while the ball skipped along the frets. To Nick's left, several people stood around a craps pit like surgeons at an operating table, watching earnestly as a pair of dice tumbled across the felt. When the dice came to rest, the players cheered, raising their arms in celebration. Suddenly, Nick felt the same disenchantment he had felt last night at his mother's house. A fretful heat rose through his body, settling in his temples. Nothing ever seemed to change in his life. For years he had lived in the same city, rented the same apartment. He kept returning home to face the same problems with his mother, and still had the same girlfriend he took for granted in the same egocentric ways. Even his job as a copy editor, the mandatory attentiveness of which he had once found challenging, had grown stale, with no opportunity for advancement. Something had to give. He would break up with Annie as soon as they got back to San Francisco—it would, after all, be the right thing to do. He turned to her and said, "You're going to be sorry you made this bet."

Just then, the wheel slowed to a stop, the ball landing in a red canoe marked with the number seven.

"Double threat," said the man. "We both win."

"I stand corrected," Nick said.

A sense of remorse poured through him as the dealer paid Annie her winnings. Nick expected her to gloat, to tell him what a naysayer he was. Instead, she looked at him with tears in her eyes.

"What is it?" he asked.

The man in the hat pushed his stacks of chips toward the dealer. "Color me up," he said.

"Annie," said Nick.

The man stood, adjusting the clasp of his tie, his new chips pressed into his palms. "Luck to you both," he said, and walked off.

Nick was glad to see him go. "Tell me what's wrong," he said, but Annie didn't speak.

They collected her money from the cashier and walked wordlessly through the casino. When they reached the Forum shops, Nick told her he was sorry for being such a pessimist.

"I want to go home," she said coarsely.

"Today?"

"Not *home* home. Back to your mom's."

He felt sheepish. "OK," he said. "If that's what you want."

As they drove south toward his mother's house, passing vacant desert lots choked with tumbleweeds, Annie looked out her window, rain streaking the glass. "I'm pregnant," she said.

At first Nick didn't respond. He gripped the steering wheel and focused on the bumper of the car in front of them, trying to process what he had heard. Annie had refused to go on the pill, claiming the progesterone gave her acne, but they always used protection. Could one of the condoms have been defective? They had sex only twice a month, every other week—a metronomic rhythm of contrived intimacy into which they had quietly settled—and condoms were something like ninety-seven percent reliable. The odds had been in their favor.

"Say something," Annie said. She held the cycling cap between her knees, her hair draped over her ears.

"How long have you known?"

"Two weeks. I should have told you sooner, but I wasn't sure how." She looked beyond him, eyes barren. "We both know this isn't something you want."

"What about you?" he said. "This is what *you* want?"

"Would that really be so terrible?"

Nick said nothing. Flatly, with an air of sufferance, Annie gave him the details. She was in the middle of her first trimester, due in autumn, and had already been to see an obstetrician. It wasn't the end of the world, she said. They wanted children at *some* point, didn't they? She was twenty-nine years old—her clock was ticking. "Better early than never."

"Pregnant," he said, as if sounding out a word he had never heard before. "How could this have happened?"

She wasn't sure, she told him, but why not make the best of it? For a second Nick wondered if he was even the father, though he knew her well enough to know she would never cheat on him—he thought so, at least. It made sense now that Annie had hardly touched her risotto last night at the restaurant, that she had ordered sparkling water over a beer or a glass of wine and had awakened this morning with an upset stomach. He gripped the steering wheel tighter. "You're right," he said. "You should have told me sooner."

◄◄--►►

That evening, his mother made them dinner, lamb chops and green beans and garlic mashed potatoes. Nick couldn't eat. He felt gut-punched, doomed, blinking down at his plate while Annie and his mother chatted like sisters, Annie telling her of the money she had won and his mother raising her glass to Annie's good fortune. Nick didn't bring up the subject of the sugar, nor did he mention his mother's medication. "I'm not feeling so hot," he announced, and went to his bedroom to lie down.

Later that night, he and Annie lay side by side in his bed. Nick rubbed her leg while she cried.

"You really don't want it, do you?" she said.

He listened to the supplication in her voice, the worry. "You don't have to have it," Nick said, as compassionately as he could. He touched his head to hers, her pillowcase wet with tears. Annie turned away from him. "There are alternatives," he said.

"Jesus."

"What?" Nick asked.

"I'm just trying to work this out." She sat up quickly. "I mean, my God."

"'This'?"

"This!" Annie shouted, moving her hand back and forth between them. "The two of us. How I ever managed to get myself here with you, to this spot in my life. How I've allowed myself to stay with you for so long." She smiled at him. "You fucker," she said. "You *shit*."

"Annie—"

"You used to be so sweet, Nick. There was always something I thought was so nice about you. So different." She cried harder now. "Who knew you'd turn out to be so goddamn . . . *fraudulent*."

"You're the one who's been secretive," Nick said weakly. He felt shamed, small inside.

"Do you think I haven't known, that I wasn't going to find out?"

"Find out what?"

"Fuck you," Annie whispered.

There was a long silence. Nick covered his face with his hands.

"Just tell me how you could treat someone this way," she said. "What's been going through your head all these years?"

"I didn't know it would come to this."

"The baby, Nick? What did you *think* it would come to? How did you think it was all going to end?"

"I don't know," he said.

Annie looked down at her hands, shaking her head. "Why," she asked him, "are you such a complete fucking prick?"

Nick lay awake for a long while, staring at the ceiling. When he was sure Annie was asleep, he rose from the bed, stepped into his tennis shoes, and put on his houndstooth duffle coat. The coat was heavy and woolen, and hung down to where his knees had stretched the threadbare flannel of his pajama bottoms. He found a flashlight in the hall closet, then slipped quietly out the kitchen door.

Though the rain had stopped, the temperature had fallen, so he fastened the coat's toggles and pulled the hood up over his head. The two mesquites that towered over his mother's backyard—planted the week he had started elementary school—forked the blackened sky with their long, naked branches. A cloud edged its way past a crescent moon, and he saw a pale grouping of stars flickering in and out of sight like some distant neon sign. The wind, to Nick, carried the smell of an old penny.

In a corner of the yard was the wooden shed his father had built years before he died—the only place Nick hadn't checked when he had searched for the sugar. It was bright red with a white gambrel roof, a barn in miniature. He unlatched the door, the hinges squealing as he opened it. Inside, the shed was dark as a cave, and he shined the flashlight over rakes and shovels, over an orange wheelbarrow and a heap of broken flagstone. Then he saw them, several boxes of

Domino sugar standing in two rows along the back wall. He counted twenty-three in all, unopened, lined shoulder to shoulder like soldiers set to march.

Nick felt a surge of despair, and for a moment he had to turn away, as if he had looked upon something gruesome, something dead. He set the flashlight on a shelf and piled the boxes into the wheelbarrow. Outside, he latched the door behind him.

A dog howled as Nick wheeled the boxes through the wrought-iron gate. He made his way across the driveway and down the sidewalk, and kept going, watching his breath funnel out from his lips, until he reached the southern edge of the development, where the Mojave opened into an ocean of darkness. Here he stopped, looking all around—in front of him the desert, behind him a shore of houses, barrack-like structures crowded into rows. He could see past the sloping development to the flat, distant valley. The city was a grid of blinking specks that resembled the components of a circuit board. It was muddy where Nick stood, so he stepped onto a large rock fringed by saltbush. He shined the flashlight into the landscape before him. Chollas grew like heads of coral from the dirt, one of them as tall as a streetlamp, a horned owl perched in its highest crotch, eyes glowing in the beam.

Tucking the flashlight beneath his arm, Nick took one of the boxes from the wheelbarrow, tore it open, and poured a small mound of sugar into his hand. The crystals were cool on his skin, sifting through his fingers like fine white sand. He spread the remainder over the rock on which he stood. One by one he tore open the boxes and scattered the sugar, as he might fistfuls of ash, onto the desert floor, tossing the empties into the night. When he finished, he heard a rustle in the distance. He aimed the beam at the giant cactus just in time to see the owl shoot from its perch.

For a second Nick lost sight of it. Then he spotted it above him, a dark form in the sky. It climbed and circled, volplaning through the air. He watched it soar away, watched it turn back in a high, graceful loop: *beautiful,* he thought. It began to dive, plummeting silently toward the earth, toward where Nick stood on the rock. Before he could move, the owl was upon him.

He heard the beating of wings, saw the flash of a beak, a talon. Ducking his head, he swung at the owl, his fingertips brushing plumage. He ran, zigzagging into the muddy desert, dodging cacti, dropping the flashlight. The animal wouldn't relent. "Dammit!" Nick cried, crouching low to the ground. He waved his arms above his head as if flagging down a plane. When he looked up, the owl was gone.

He walked back toward the wheelbarrow, feeling his neck and his face, checking for blood. He found the flashlight and shined it over his arms, his hands. His coat was undamaged. There wasn't a scratch on him. He had never heard of an owl attacking a human unprovoked, and he figured that in some way it had felt threatened, mistaking him for a predator. Nick looked down to find his legs were shivering—not from the cold but from some sort of rush. He was deeply saddened by his argument with Annie; at the same time, he felt ignited by a classi- fied knowledge of the world, of its hazards and surprises, and could hardly wait to share his story of the owl. The thought occurred to him that it would sound like a lie.

A gust of wind roused the branches of a menodora shrub, a noise like the rattle of a maraca. Far away, he heard what sounded like hoot- ing, and he wondered if the owl was on its way back. That it had come after him in the first place was a portent—Nick was sure—though of what he didn't know. He listened until he heard nothing at all.

When he got back, lights were on inside the house. Nick closed the kitchen door behind him, took off his coat, and stepped out of his mud- caked tennis shoes. He went into the living room, where his mother, looking startled, sat cross-legged in the center of the couch. On her lap was a plastic storage box filled with framed photographs of his father. In the short time that Nick had been out, she had removed most of them from the tables and shelves, from the mantle. On the walls, shadow-like rectangles of varying sizes designated where frames had hung, the wallpaper faded around them. He saw that she had disposed of the chrysanthemums: the vase stood empty on the windowsill.

"You scared me," she said. "It's past midnight."

"I needed some air," Nick said. "I had some thinking to do."

She didn't say anything.

"What's all this?" he asked.

"I want them out of here," his mother said. "I can't have them in this house anymore." She hugged one of the frames to her chest as if to bid it farewell. "Whatever you're going to say," she told him, "keep it to yourself. Just let me have this, Nicky. Let me have this one thing."

He nodded. "Sure," he said. "OK."

She placed the frame in the box, folding her hands together, touching her knuckles to her lips. "I had a dream about him earlier. The funny thing is, I can't remember what happened. I've forgotten already, can you believe that? But I woke up. I looked around the room for him, knowing he was there somewhere."

"A bad dream?" he asked.

"Oh. It was a good one, I think." She stared at him. "I'm not crazy," she said.

"No."

He remembered that at his father's wake his mother had taken photographs of the body, standing over the casket in a kind of trance, snapping one after another as Nick looked on from the other side of the room. After the burial she stayed in bed for weeks, watching soap operas and eating Ferrara Pan candies—Red Hots and Lemonheads and Atomic Fire Balls and Boston Baked Beans—the little boxes piled on her nightstand. She was no better now, he thought, than she had been back then.

She looked down at her robe, spooling the belt around her thumb. "I'm sorry for us," his mother said, something desperate in her voice.

"Well."

"Tell me I'll get through this, Nicky."

"Mom."

"Tell me."

"You'll get through it," he said, but he wasn't sure she ever would. "We both will."

She held her head in her hands, her hair pressed flat. "When I would go out with your father, to cocktail parties or dinner parties, I'd look across a room and see him there, talking to someone, sipping his drink, and I'd feel so safe." She took a breath. "Before he got sick," she said, setting the storage box on the carpet. "I don't think I'll ever feel that safe again, Nick, not in this life or the next." His mother wiped her eyes, then began to tug at her wedding ring. As she worked it over the fat of her knuckle, Nick watched the skin turn white and bubble out, as though it might pop. When the ring finally, miraculously, came off, she held it out like a prize. "Yours," she said. "Take it."

"What are you talking about?"

"I want you to have it," she said. She quirked her eyebrows. "For Annie, or someone else. I don't want it anymore."

"We're not engaged, Mom."

"Maybe not," she said.

The band had tarnished over the years, but as his mother held the ring, the diamond glittered like new.

"This is nuts," Nick said. "That was from Dad."

She cocked her head.

"What," he said.

"It's yours now, sweetheart."

Nick felt nauseated. Something impelled him to step forward, and with a shaky hand he took the ring. He turned it around in his palm, his heart rising in his chest. He had a feeling of weightlessness, as though, like a helium balloon, he might float away. He thought of

Annie asleep in his bed, of the fetus growing inside her. Nick had done what he had sworn he would never do: he had hurt her. He despised himself for suggesting she terminate the pregnancy, remembering a time before he had met her, long before his father had died and his mother had begun to self-destruct, when Nick had moved through his days with a sense of freedom and possibility, when he'd had to consider no one but himself. That time, as foreign to him as anything, was gone forever. He was older now, a different person. He was going to be a father. The word lodged in his mind, and he thought of the man in the Stetson, of his covetable smugness, of the contentment with which he had spoken of his wife. Nick thought of how everything was going to change in the next seven and a half months, whether he liked it or not. For a moment it excited him, the idea of a family, his own. He hoped Annie was still in love with him; that he wasn't in love with her suddenly seemed beside the point. He could commit himself to her for good, to her alone, to her hats and her wasteful spending and her starry-eyed visions of the future. In time, he might even grow to feel for her the way she had always felt for him. He could make it work, this new chapter of his life, but even as he decided this—even as Nick was almost able to imagine Annie as his wife—he knew how difficult it was going to be, how terribly difficult, and he pressed his mother's ring between his thumb and forefinger as if to crush it like a grape.

"Thank you," he said.

"Go back to sleep," she told him.

When Nick returned to bed, Annie was awake, combing her fingers through her hair. He kissed her forehead, her chin, the bridge of her nose. He said nothing, sliding his hand between her legs. At first she resisted, pushing at his chest, his arms. "Asshole," she whispered. But he continued to kiss her, and slowly her muscles slackened, welcoming him.

"I'm sorry," Nick said. They moved against each other. He let out a groan, inside her now, the ring clenched in his fist. "I'm sorry."

He looked into Annie's eyes and tried to recall what had first drawn him to her, what had brought them together so many years ago. She shuddered beneath him, and his mind slipped back to the present. "I've got you," he said.

Lying beside her, he placed a hand to her stomach. Through the open blinds he could see gray clouds floating in the sky like ships on an ink-black sea. Wind pressed gently at the window.

"I'm keeping it," she said.

"Of course you are."

"Our baby," Annie said, her stomach tightening beneath his fingers.

"That's right," he said.

"Ours."

In his other hand Nick held the ring. He listened to Annie's breathing, to the house as it ticked softly in the darkness. Outside, the moon was a rind of white light, girdled by the clouds. Tomorrow they would board a plane and fly back to San Francisco, leaving his mother behind. Her welfare, her survival, was up to her now—he had his own life to deal with. Autumn would arrive before they knew it. There were so many things to discuss, so many decisions to be made. Annie laid a hand over his—cautiously, it seemed—and he felt the light warmth of her palm. He gave in to her touch, letting her guide his fingers back and forth across her stomach. He wanted to tell her of the owl, of how it had swooped down, for no apparent reason, to assault him, of how he had gotten away unscathed. He wanted to tell her the only thing she needed to hear: that she was his one true love, that she always would be.

"Ours," he said.

First Sight

We're not the people I thought we were.

I'm hiding among the branches of a honeysuckle shrub, watching you through a space of light where the vertical blinds don't quite meet the sill of your lover's bedroom window. Your foot hangs lazily off the bed, a beige sock gathered around your ankle. Propped on an elbow, he runs his fingertips down the slope of your thigh, spiders them over your knee. Clothing litters the carpet: his white oxford shirt, your floral-print blouse, the navy corduroys that caught his foot as he hurried out of them, the designer blue jeans I gave you on your thirty-ninth birthday, a year ago tomorrow. A nightstand lamp illuminates your bodies. He slides his hand beneath your leg, thumbing the rise of your calf, skin that I, too, have touched though never appreciated. For a crazy moment, my stomach tight with envy, I wish I were on the other side of the glass, the three of us together—to share you would be enough. Sadness or anger, unease of a different sort, might prompt me to confront him, to ring his doorbell and tell him who I am. But I'm not sad and I'm not angry. I've never loved you.

147

Outside, a sickle moon shines through a high film of clouds. I'm standing just beyond his cedar-picket fence, at the side of his single-story tract house. Twin pine trees loom over the low-pitched roof and their limbs joggle in the wind. At my feet, a dusting of snow stirs in miniature twisters. It's the first Friday of a bitter Las Vegas March, the temperature a record low, but when the air gentles, ebbing like a tide, I can almost feel the heat of your body against mine, imagining myself in his place. Like you, he's still wearing socks, though his are black with gold toes. Neither of you thought to remove them. I watched, coveting your eagerness, as you both kicked off your shoes, pulled off your clothes, as you fell, embracing, onto the bed. Like a child taking an interest in a toy only after another child plays with it, I saw you in a new way as he made love to you. I held my breath, unable to move, wanting, finally, what for years I've rejected.

It's true, Annie. For the first time, I want you. It feels something like nerves, a trembling heaviness that has me staked out in the cold, breaking the law, degrading myself: I'm not a voyeur by habit.

Still, it's desire alone that keeps me here. There are risks to watching your wife with another man, and if I were any kind of husband I might have considered them. But I risk nothing, my heart unbroken. He stretches out across the comforter, and you place your hand in his. You nuzzle up to him. A smile opens across your face. I can see how much he means to you, Annie, and I'm moved only by an erotic excitement the likes of which I've never known before.

At the same time, I find myself consumed with guilt. When I think of your unrequited feelings for me, of how lonely you seem when we're together, of what it might be like to be you, Annie—to yearn for your own spouse's attention, to know the boundaries of your own appeal—I hate myself for ever agreeing to marry you. This morning, when for the first time in years it snowed—a light, whorling snow that floated through the atmosphere like the white tufts of cottonwood seeds—I held my head and cried. You were still asleep, and I sat alone at our kitchen table, watching the flakes spin by the window, an odd, miraculous sight, an omen of indeterminate significance. I wondered, as I often do, how your life would have turned out had you married someone else.

And now you've found him, my replacement. He scratches his stomach, opens and closes his legs. He lifts your hand and kisses the side of your thumb. I'm surprised he's not a handsome man. You're as attractive as you were the day we met, clean-limbed with a luminous smile, your golden hair collected in the tight chignon you've come to wear in recent years. You're beautiful, Annie, and I'm sorry it's taken me so long to truly realize it. But he's balding, and what hair he has, thin and reddish, floats electrostatically around his ears. He has a wide nose, a prominent Adam's apple, a cluster of birthmarks in the center of his chest. I can't help thinking you can do better.

I step away from the window to look around for neighbors, anyone who might catch sight of me. Thimbles of snow cap the peaks of his fence. The air, moving between the honeysuckle's flowerless branches, smells of wet pine needles and the wood smoke that drifts from two chimneys up the block. Over the fence, slender poplars border his driveway, and their boughs sway in the wind. A Neighborhood Watch sign hangs from a streetlamp at the edge of his lawn.

I wish I could summon some type of normal reaction, Annie, something other than envy and guilt. I wish I could at least grant you that.

The Neighborhood Watch sign rattles against its brackets, a sound like a train running slowly over tracks. The streetlamp blinks erratically, as if transmitting a coded message, orange light dappling the sidewalk.

When he gets up from the bed, half an hour later, you hold out a hand. He pulls you to your feet, each of you dressing though remaining shoeless. Together you leave the room, and together, after a short time, you return. He's carrying a corkscrew, forks, and a plate of spaghetti, leftovers, I suppose, microwaved. A bottle of red wine is tucked beneath his arm. Behind him, you hold the empty bowl of a wineglass in each hand. You settle in next to each other, like guests at a hotel, for an intimate dinner in bed.

Thinking the movement might warm me, I jog in place, rock back and forth on my heels, canvas sneakers soaked to the laces. I zip my coat to my chin, slip my gloved hands into the pockets. In one of them is a small wrapped box, solid and rectangular between my fingers. The box contains a silver necklace, from which hangs a pair of tiny red dice, each one a carved ruby pendant. I bought it for you, Annie, the day before we were married, nearly a decade ago. Strange as it seems, I've carried the necklace in my billfold ever since, knotted in a clump beneath my driver's license. Every so often I take it out. I untie the knots and loop the necklace around my thumbs. I rotate the dice between my fingertips as though they're the evidence of some ancient, unsolved crime.

I've gotten you dozens of other gifts over the years—watches and earrings and bracelets—none of which I've grown attached to. I can't say why I've been unable to part with this one. Now, after all this time, I've decided to give it to you, tomorrow, on your fortieth birthday. The necklace is yours, Annie, and I want you to have it. Earlier today, I offered a downtown jeweler ten dollars to box and wrap it for me, a woman with wrinkled skin and soft green eyes, who handled the necklace as if it were the most valuable item in her store. I had just left the magazine for the day, my column complete, and I was feeling good, high on the sense of accomplishment I get when I meet my weekly deadline. The woman wrapped the box in shiny pink paper and tied it with a black ribbon. She wouldn't take the money, nodding as she patted my hand.

It was while I was driving home, stuck in traffic on Las Vegas

Boulevard, that I spotted the two of you arm-in-arm in front of Bellagio, standing at the edge of the artificial lake. I made a U-turn and pulled the Accord over across the street. I rolled down my window. In the gray dusk light, you watched like a couple of tourists as the half-hourly fountain show began, acres of dancing water choreographed to "Singin' in the Rain," white light shining from beneath the surface, mist carried on the wind. You tickled his chin as he clapped to the music. I couldn't believe it was you, Annie, you with another man.

I switched on my hazard lights and watched for what seemed like hours. You were in the middle of a crowd, on the far side of a six-lane boulevard, and I could only see your back. I started to wonder if I had mistaken another woman for my wife. After all, you were supposed to be at work. You told me, Annie, that you had taken a double shift, the evening and the graveyard. You told me that you would be covering for another cocktail waitress—Deborah, the one who always invites you to happy hour when you're off before six o'clock, the one who's always asking for favors. I believed you: you're not known to lie. Never mind that every time I've stopped by the Tropicana to say hello Deborah is on her break, or out to lunch, or out sick with some peculiar new illness.

Dark slush spurted from tires as automobiles veered around me. The song ended, and the two of you walked along the lake toward the entrance of the casino. I made another U-turn at the light, and when I pulled into the valet-parking lane, I saw you sitting beside him on a bench, your face lowered against the wind. Ducking my head, I shifted the Accord into reverse. I watched from a distance, squinting over the steering wheel, your birthday gift in my coat pocket, Annie.

Visitors thronged the entrance. They emerged from taxis with backpacks and suitcases as bellmen rushed about. After a time, a white BMW pulled up. Where, I wondered, was your Volkswagen? He tipped the attendant while you walked around to the other side of the car. To everyone there but me, the two of you must have looked like husband and wife, a happily married couple. As though to encourage this impression, he leaned in to kiss you before driving away. A thrill quivered through me as I followed.

A wedding photograph, an 8 x 10 in a large wooden frame, hangs on the wall beside the door, him in a black tuxedo, a dark-haired woman in a white strapless gown, and I start to wonder about his marriage. Do they have any children? Does he love his wife? Where is she, Annie? Out with friends? Away for the weekend? When will she return? He's made no effort to put away her things. A leather purse hangs from the doorknob. Matching dressers of equal height stand on either side of the room, and on one of them is a chrome eyelash curler, a tampon still in its wrapper, a pearl bracelet. On the carpet below the bed, next to your favorite black loafers and the red duffel bag you always carry with you to the gym, is a pair of gold heels, toes facing out, positioned like slippers. But I can see that he's not wearing his wedding ring, Annie, and only now do I notice that you're not wearing yours.

I think about the weekend we eloped, our road trip from San Francisco in your old Jeep Wrangler. You had only been to Las Vegas once, and you wanted to see more of the city in which I had grown up. You wanted the ceremony to be performed in a wedding chapel, "just like in the movies," you said. This was six years before we decided to make Las Vegas our home. You were five months' pregnant, still queasy and hungry all the time, but you insisted it would be more leisurely if we took the Jeep. Off and on during the nine-hour journey, as we cruised south through Los Banos and Lemoore, through Avenal and Bakersfield and Barstow, you held my hand while I drove.

I had decided not to let my mother know we were coming, afraid of how she might react when I told her we had married in secret, when she saw that you were pregnant. I was only thinking of you,

Annie. I didn't want to add to the strain of our relationship: we both knew I had only agreed to marry you because of the baby. I couldn't understand why you still loved me, why you told me so almost every day, and that weekend I hoped I could find a way to apologize for everything I had ever done to make you feel unwanted.

We had booked a room at Treasure Island, at the north end of the Strip. Pirates and wenches greeted visitors at the main entrance, men in red bandanas and tight striped T-shirts, women in skimpy dirndls with elaborate hems. Other men wore eye patches and leather vests, and stumbled around near one of the bars hoisting jugs in imitation of rum-blitzed buccaneers. In line at the reception desk, I made conversation with the woman in front of me while you played nickel slots back in the casino.

She was a purchasing agent, in town for a convention. She had dark skin and long brown hair and eyes the gray-blue color of silt. I smiled as she poked fun at my hometown. "Skin City," she called it, "Lost Wages." She wore black leather pants and a tight aquamarine sweater. She licked her lips and wound the sleeve of the sweater around her finger. "Nick," I said, and as we shook hands I knew I would see her again.

That night, after an evening of blackjack and roulette—after we had lost all the money we had set aside for gambling, Annie—I lay awake while you slept, combing my fingers through my hair, contemplating the future. I dressed in a T-shirt and swimming trunks and wrapped a towel around my waist. I rode the elevator downstairs and made my way through the casino and outside to the pool, hoping to clear my mind. It was past midnight and the June air was heavy and warm. All around, palm trees towered over topiary shrubs trimmed as anchors and parrots. Empty of swimmers and lit by underwater bulbs, the pool glowed like a phosphorescent tide, and I cut the surface in an easy breaststroke. The water, for some reason, was startlingly cold, but when I reached the middle I turned onto my back and floated with my arms and legs extended, as though reclining in an open field. I closed my eyes, acclimating as I drifted. When I opened them, the woman from the reception line was standing at the edge of the pool in an orange bikini. A blue robe lay in a heap behind her.

"Hi again," she said. "Mind if I join you?"

"I've got to warn you," I said, wading to the side. "The water's cold as hell."

Her long legs were as shapely as I had imagined them, her stomach flat as a sheet pulled tightly across a mattress. She raised her arms into the air and took flight over my head, entering the water in a spread-legged dive and gliding along the bottom of the pool. She rose to the surface and shook her hair from her neck.

"Did you see me come out here?" I asked.

I assumed she had come upon me by coincidence, but a part of me wondered if her appearance had been calculated, the result, however unlikely, of some kind of spying.

A grin lit her face. "I had you followed."

We made small talk, her teeth chattering as the water lapped our shoulders. After a while, she asked me if I had a girlfriend, and I said that I did. Wet bangs clung to her forehead and drops of water trickled down her skin. I couldn't keep from envisioning her naked in her room. She moved nearer, and her leg glanced the back of my hand.

"Let me ask you something," I said. "Have you ever been in love?"

"Let me ask *you* something—Nick, is it?" She shivered at my side. I could smell alcohol—gin, maybe—on her breath. "Why are we still in this pool?"

I laughed.

"Let's go," she said, nodding toward the hotel.

I imagined what it would be like to kiss her, to slide a hand into her bikini bottom. It had been a while since the last time I had been unfaithful to you, Annie; I was making an effort to be a better partner, a better person. Still, with nervous fingers I reached out and touched her arm. I brought her to me, feeling her nipples against my chest. I knew I could have done anything I wanted. But I couldn't stop thinking about you. I couldn't stop picturing your face. I backed away.

"What is it?" she said.

"I can't do this," I told her.

I thought that maybe, then and there, I had fallen for you. But it wasn't love that I felt.

"I get it," she said, folding her arms over her stomach. "I understand."

She slipped into her robe, and I toweled off. I stood staring at a row of giant casino signs, visible above the high fronds, lined up like dominoes and shining warmly over the Strip. *I'm going to marry a woman I'm not even attracted to*, I thought, *a woman I'm not in love with. I'm going to be a father.* There was an immeasurable range of ways a life could unfold, I figured, and this was how mine was unfolding. I decided that what I knew of myself amounted to little more than what I knew of anything. Between the signs, Annie, I could see your blue eyes staring through the night.

"At what point did I lose control?" I said, not really meaning to.

"Look," she said. "We can just grab a drink."

But I turned, apologizing, and walked off.

Back in the casino, I found my way to one of the gift shops. It must have been after one o'clock. The shop was empty except for two women paging through magazines toward the back. I looked through souvenir shot glasses, snow globes, coffee mugs, searching for the perfect item: a gift, whimsical but nice, for my soon-to-be wife. Finally, something beside the sales counter caught my eye. In a long display case was an arrangement of silver necklaces, hanging from which were intricate little pendants shaped as slot machines and casino chips and roulette wheels, each one impossibly small, carved from emeralds, sapphires, and diamonds. The dice gleamed red in the middle of the arrangement, the only pair in the case. The clerk opened it with a key, and I lifted the necklace by its clasp. I held it in front of my face, tapping the ruby dice with my fingernail.

It was an expensive gift, but I bought it anyway. We were to marry the next morning. It would be a momentous day, Annie, and I wanted the necklace to commemorate it.

Three hours later, the wind has calmed, though the temperature, it seems, has dropped. A little while ago, I drove to a nearby Wendy's, where I ate alone in the Accord. When I returned, the two of you were still in bed, still sipping wine, still talking and laughing as you are now, the sauce-stained plate resting on the carpet, the wine bottle standing between his legs. It seems to me, Annie, that it's been years since we've had such a long conversation. I'm trying to recall one, a deep-felt talk that wound on for hours, but nothing comes to mind.

Before long, the glasses and the bottle are on the carpet too, and you're leaning over him, kissing his lower lip, smoothing your fingers over the hairless summit of his head. You undress each other even faster than you did the first time. He turns you over, placing a hand around your breast, and you take him between your legs. Your mouth falls open as he probes for entrance.

I pull off my gloves and stuff them into the pockets of my coat. I unzip my pants. Again I imagine myself in his place, the sound of your breath in my ear, the salty flavor of your skin, the gamy smell of sex, and all at once my muscles constrict. You wrap your legs around his waist, and he reaches back and grabs hold of your ankles, thumbs pressed to the balls of your feet. Then an increase in tempo. A series of rhythmic thrusts. A sudden, jerky finish that coincides with my own.

You lie in his arms now, Annie, your legs wishboned beneath the sheet, the comforter bunched at the foot of the bed. He stares at the ceiling with triumphant satisfaction. I zip my pants, breathing heavily. Whenever you work the graveyard shift, you call the house around this time to check in, say good night, and I wonder if you've forgotten. He says something and you slap his wrist. You cup your hand over your mouth, your face wrenched with laughter. He reaches over you and switches off the lamp.

A page from a magazine, *Las Vegas Weekly*, I realize, is lying beneath the honeysuckle, spread flat under an awning of branches. I look to see if it contains my column, but it's only the Personals page. In the paltry light from his window, I can just make out the print. "Lonely Divorcé Seeks Soul Mate," reads one of the ads, followed by "Narcissistic Solipsist Searching For Something Real." A motorcycle passes in the distance, its gears shifting with a low swallow. I'm thinking that it's been six months since we've shared a bed, since I've held you in my arms.

Back in the Accord, I start the engine and set the heater to high. I can see his house in the headlights, halfway up the block, his BMW parked in the driveway. It's a little before midnight, and my plan is to head home, but I can't get myself to drive away. What else am I hoping to see here? What am I looking for?

I fear that if you leave me I'll let pass the only person who's ever held me dear, and that if you remain my wife I might never find the courage to let you go. I've kept you at a distance since the very beginning, Annie. I've cheated and I've lied. But you've rarely complained, and I'm ashamed to say I'm grateful for it. As I labored for years over a novel I would never finish, ignoring our relationship in pursuit of a dream, you were a constant source of encouragement. When I resented you for getting pregnant, you graciously forgave me. And when my mother died, still grief-stricken and still alone fifteen years after my father's death—only six months after we moved from San Francisco to care for her, her health failing, her mental faculties not far behind—you held me as I cried. Until today, I found comfort in your loyalty and your predictability. What, I wonder, will become of us now?

I switch off the headlights and his house disappears. I slide the seat as far back as it will go, kick my feet up on the dash, and close my eyes.

When I wake, the engine is still running and the orange needle of the fuel gauge is leaning toward empty. Shapes are emerging in the pre-dawn light. I didn't intend to sleep as long as I have. The heater has been going for hours, and I can feel sweat on my upper lip. My sneakers are dry. My neck and my legs are stiff and pulsating.

I step out of the car, shaking in the air's cold embrace, and relieve myself in the gutter. I walk up the block, climb quietly over the waist-high fence. I see you bent before your red duffel bag, Annie, the bedsheet wrapped around you like a cape. I watch as you remove the elastic miniskirt and frilly V-neck top of your uniform, and I realize that you're planning to dress for work before returning home.

Across the room, he appears in the doorway wearing a white robe and white slippers. His rim of hair is tousled from sleep. He sits you down on the bed and places your hands over your eyes. Then he reaches into a front pocket of the robe and brings forth a small brown box. As though he's about to propose, he kneels down and places it in your lap. You lower your hands, steal a glance at him. You open the box.

The necklace glimmers in the low light of the nightstand lamp, thread-thin—gold, it appears. Hanging from it is a heart-shaped pendant the size of a postage stamp. You open the clasp, and he takes the necklace and drapes it over your chest. You stand, holding the bedsheet loosely around you, and walk to a mirror that hangs above one of the dressers. You pass a hand over the necklace, cheeks flushed,

smiling at your reflection. Behind you, he wags his eyebrows, and you
turn and kiss him on the lips.

I take the wrapped box from my pocket, turning it over a few
times before untying the ribbon and tearing away the paper. I open
it, and the lid props up firmly. The box is like a little velvet casket in
my hand. The dice look silly, small. I'm embarrassed by the sight of
them. *Dice*, I think. *Dice on a necklace.*

I toss the box and shove the necklace in my pocket, clenching
my teeth so hard it hurts. When I look up, you're no longer there.
I watch him pick through a drawer of sweaters, and a second later
I'm thinking of our baby boy, of how he looked the moment he was
born—nothing like a baby at all, really—swollen and motionless,
purple-faced, slick-skinned, like a fetal pig wet with formaldehyde.
I remember the word the doctor kept using—*complications*—and the
silence that fell over the delivery room as I turned to you, squeezing
your hand, and the way you stared at me, as though your eyes might
never blink again.

Why didn't you leave me then, Annie? Why didn't I leave you?
What is it that's kept us together all these years?

He's still deciding on a sweater, and I consider keying the hood
of his BMW, stuffing a rock in the tailpipe, letting the air out of the
tires. Instead, I step back, cocking my leg like a pitcher, and put my
heel through his fence. I do it over and over, snapping the pickets
like tree branches. Each kick is weaker than the last, and by the time
I'm on the fourth or fifth picket it's like I'm kicking at a cinder-block
wall. When I stop, it feels as if I've sprained my ankle. There's a tear
in the side of my sneaker, a few long splinters sticking from my sock
like needles in a pincushion. Shards of rust-colored cedar stand out
against the gray-white snow.

I know he's heard the commotion, and when I turn around, panting, the blinds are parted and his robe is pressed against the sill. His
eyes are squinted. His breath is clouding the glass.

I climb over the fence, hoping it won't collapse, feeling like an idiot and a coward, and limp back to the Accord. No sooner have I started the engine than his front door opens and he comes scuttling through the snow in his slippers. His robe falls open to reveal a swath of pale inner leg. He's carrying a baseball bat and wearing a look that tells me I'll drive away if I know what's good for me. But I don't. I sit here, as still as when I first watched him make love to you, and in the shrinking space between us, over the flat length of sidewalk, I can see the last nine years of my life, our entire marriage laid before me like a strip of film, frame after frame of days and weeks and months, of birthdays and holidays and anniversaries. I start to feel a little sick, paralyzed by the knowledge that I've made a mess of a good thing, by the aching awareness that I need you to love me, Annie, even though I've never loved you in return.

When he raises the bat, poised to bring it down over the windshield, I don't move. I close my eyes and wait for the impact, the sound of aluminum crashing through glass, but it never comes. I open them to find the bat lowered at his side. I can tell he knows who I am.

I turn off the engine, expecting you to emerge, wrapped in the bedsheet, from his front door. You're still inside, though, and it's your absence, somehow, that emboldens me. Slowly, making a show of it, I place the keys on the dash, and we just stare at one another. Half of me wants to get out and face him, bat or no bat. But I keep staring, until, after a minute or so, he turns and walks back toward the house. He moves slowly, the bat trailing behind him, tracing a drunken line through the snow.

As he reaches his doorway, he looks over his shoulder and nods. Because I know what he's thinking, because it's the same thing I'm thinking—that our encounter will remain a secret, that it will be ours alone to puzzle out—I nod back. He closes the door, and in the lingering silence I get the sense that I'm being watched, not by you or him or any of his neighbors, but by some intangible presence that's privy to my feelings, some piece of me, it seems, that I left behind. And what I feel, what I realize, Annie, is that our life together will carry on. That there are things we learn to live with so as not to lose what we can't live without. That I owe you more than my loyalty and my love: I owe you my respect.

Over the mountains to the east, a gossamer plane of clouds is beginning to separate, an open strip of sky brightening to blue. I start the engine, and the sun inches over the horizon, sending a warm glow across the land. The poplars along his driveway cast willowy shadows, and everything is covered by a skin of snow, everything dormant in the bright winter daybreak.

I take the necklace from my pocket, hang it around the neck of the rearview mirror, unsure of what I'll do with it—unsure of what my gift to you will be. When I pull away from the curb, the dice sway like a hypnotist's charm.

It's still warm inside the car, so I crack the window. Even now, with the sun shining, the air has a bite to it, breezing in as I drive south toward home, but it feels good on my face, like a splash of aftershave or ice-cold water. My ankle is throbbing, and I step lightly on the accelerator, minding the fuel gauge. Again I think back to that night long ago. When I returned to our room, you were still asleep, and for a while, in the near-dark, I stood watching you, glad that I hadn't gone any farther with the woman from the reception line. I crept to the closet and held the necklace to the white lace dress you planned to wear to the chapel the next day, just to see how they would look together. I pictured us at the altar, vows spoken, rings on our fingers. We were going to start a family. I whispered your name, praying that something in me would change.

Soon the temperature will rise, the snow will melt. Tonight we'll celebrate your birthday, Annie. We'll share a bed, husband and wife. I'll hold you in my arms and we'll talk for hours.

Crash Site on a Desert Mountain Outside Las Vegas

I WAS HIKING WITH MY FATHER IN THE DESERT OUTSIDE LAS Vegas, up the eastern face of Mount Potosi, not far from where Carole Lombard had died in a plane crash more than forty years earlier. The trail cut through a dense landscape of cottonwoods and Apache plume, past limestone cliffs and steep, rocky hillsides, winding along the belly of a shallow canyon that ran like a scar up the front of the mountain. Sunlight speared through the branches as we took turns swigging from my father's canteen, an old stainless-steel one he'd had since his years in the Army. "Warm today," he said, and when he turned around it looked like he was crying.

What appeared to be tears were only drops of sweat, running from his forehead into the corners of his eyes, spilling down his cheeks. It occurred to me that I had seen my father cry only once, when we were wrestling in the living room a few weeks before and I elbowed him in the nose, breaking the lenses of his glasses—blood pouring from his nostrils, his eyes watering. He hadn't cried at my grandfather's burial, and he hadn't cried the day I watched him shred his ankle with a hedge trimmer in our backyard, and according to my mother, my father hadn't cried the morning I was born, even though he told her I was the most beautiful thing he had ever seen in this world. For a long time I had assumed that only children were allowed to cry—children and women, maybe, because my mother cried all the time.

"Thank God for this shade," my father said, coughing into his fist, gasping as he wiped the sweat from his face. He pawed through a low tangle of branches and we emerged into a clearing where a camouflage hunting cap lay in the shade of a yucca.

"Looks like somebody lost this," he said. The cap was faded and worn, its bill creased down the middle. He picked it up, dusted it off, set it down on the spiny limb of a fallen Joshua tree. My father was the sort of man who didn't mind going out of his way to return a lost wallet to its rightful owner.

"What if it belongs to someone who lives out here?" I said. "A homeless person, or a runaway, living in a box in the desert."

My father cocked his head the way he did when he was pretending to consider something he knew was unlikely. I had never seen any homeless in the desert, but exploring the narrow trails that twisted through the chollas behind our house, I often came across the remnants of what I assumed were their drunken overnights—cigarette butts, broken whiskey bottles, tattered sheets and old brown shoes, every now and then a soiled condom or a faded copy of *Penthouse*—and it was rumored that somewhere deep in the Mojave was an entire community of freight hoppers and gypsies and other itinerants who came and went along a secret road and slept in shanties made of ocotillo branches and aluminum cans.

"I wouldn't mind living on this mountain," I said. "I'd drink water from a cactus if I got thirsty. I'd eat snakes and lizards. I'd do whatever I wanted."

It had been only a few months since my father had received his diagnosis. I still had trouble remembering the official name of the disease: idiopathic pulmonary fibrosis, words that, whenever my mother said them, seemed to describe something exotic but innocuous that might resemble a double helix when sketched on a blackboard, not the debilitating illness that was to take my father's life in the next several years. He wasn't supposed to be hiking up mountains, even in the fair weather of autumn, but he insisted on remaining active, rolling his eyes when my mother pleaded with him to rest. He regarded his condition as though it were a rumor. At night in my bed, I tried my best not to cry, entertaining fantasies of running away from home, living by myself on the streets or in the desert. I was fourteen and didn't know much about anything.

"Not every cactus holds enough water to drink," my father said. "You'd die out here. Believe me."

It was rare that he was wrong about something, and his new voice, dry and wispy from the coughing fits that reddened his forehead and purpled his lips, was at odds with my impression of him as a figure of authority. People seemed to respect my father, talking kindly of him when he wasn't around. The only person I had ever seen challenge him was my mother, who sometimes spoke to him as if he were a child. Lately, though—ever since he had been diagnosed, failing to cry even then—she had been nothing but affectionate toward him, holding his hand in public, resting her head on his shoulder while they watched television in the evenings.

My father nudged the hunting cap with the toe of his boot, sliding the canteen into his backpack. "Shall we?"

"Let's try and find that crash site," I said.

He checked the trail guide, gasping again, breathing heavily. "We're pretty close, I think."

We had been hiking for over an hour, and I knew he was exhausted. I wasn't sure he could go much farther, but I was young and thoughtless and I wanted to see where the plane had gone down. I wanted to see where the movie star had died.

-<-->->-

Half an hour later we reached the site. It was a DC-3 that had exploded into the mountainside, sending a roiling cloud of fire into the dark winter sky—January 16th, 1942. I had read about the crash in the trail guide during the drive from the city, heading west in my father's new Buick LeSabre. In addition to Carole Lombard, the plane had been carrying her mother, fifteen soldiers, and an MGM publicist named Otto Winkler.

"This is it," my father said.

The larger sections of the plane—what had remained of the body and the wings—had been removed a long time ago, but the area was strewn with rubber hoses, twisted wire, shards of glass, and bits of crushed aluminum. We saw rusted safety pins, molten buttons shining like obsidian in the warm noon light. What looked like part of an engine had become one with the mountain: a corroded, doily-shaped thing lodged in a sheet of rock. Everywhere, the dirt was pitted with holes—dug, my father said, by treasure hunters looking for Carole Lombard's wedding ring. Clark Gable, her husband at the time of her death, had offered a reward for it, but her left hand had never been found.

"Look at all this stuff," I said.

"Don't touch anything," my father told me, his eyes slitted against the sun. "Leave everything exactly the way it is. This is sacred ground, Nick."

It was eerily silent. A high saddle of rock hung above us, and all around were big green century plants growing in clusters beneath a blue umbrella of sky. For several minutes neither of us said a word. It dawned on me that this might be our final hiking trip together, but it seems to me now that I was unwilling to believe it. My father sat on a pile of white talus rock, staring at the site in a mournful sort of way, as though it had been his own friends or relatives who had perished in the crash. I loved him, of course. The thought of his eventual disappearance from my life gave me a feeling of being chased—made my heart race, my breath quicken. I knew that he loved me too—I was his son, his only child—and that I weighed heavily on his mind when he considered the probability of his untimely death.

He kept sitting there, kept staring. Something had come over him, I could tell. I could have said any number of things to my father then, but there was a self-centered, irrational part of me that hated him for being sick, a part of me that wanted to make him cry again, the way I had in our living room a few weeks before, and so I told him, in that strange pocket of silence, the worst thing I could think of: that I wouldn't miss him when he was gone. The words slipped heedlessly from my mouth, completely unwarranted, unrelated to anything we had been talking about—untrue.

"What?" my father said. "What did you just say?"

I pictured my mother as a widow, draped in black, and then I thought back to the hunting cap we had come upon, trying to imagine what life might be like out here, alone on a desert mountain. Anger churned inside me.

"Why would you say that, Nick?" My father looked at me, his face hardened. "Why would you tell me something like that?" he asked, but I didn't answer him. I had no idea.

Sure enough, he began to cry, lowering his head, pressing his hand over his mouth. For a moment he looked as if he were in great physical pain. It was nothing I wanted to see.

I knew I had to apologize, but I couldn't speak. I couldn't even cry. I just stood there, ashamed of what I had done, wondering who I was and who I might become.